Northumbria Healthcare
NHS Foundation Trust

Patient Library Service

Please return books via **Hospital Volunteer Service** or to any of the following **Trust libraries**

Education Centre Libraries:

Hexham General Hospital, Hexham, NE46 1QJ

North Tyneside General Hospital, Rake Lane, NE29 8NH

NSECH, Northumbria Way, Cramlington, NE23 6NZ

Wansbeck General Hospital, Woodhorn Lane, NE63 9JJ

Telephone: 01434 655420 / 0191 2932761 / 01670 529665

THE SPACE-BORN

Jay West was a killer — he had to be. No human kindness could swerve him from duty, because the ironclad law of the Space Ship was that no one — *no one* — ever must live past forty! But how could he fulfil his next assignment — the murder of his sweetheart's father? Yet, how could he *not* do it? The old had to make way for the new generations. There was no air, no food, and no room for the old . . .

E. C. TUBB

THE SPACE-BORN

Complete and Unabridged

LINFORD
Leicester

First published in Great Britain

First Linford Edition
published 2008

British Library CIP Data

Tubb, E. C.
 The space-born.—Large print ed.—
Linford mystery library
1. Dystopias
2. Large type books
I. Title
823.9'14 [F]

ISBN 978–1–84782–303–8

Published by
F. A. Thorpe (Publishing)
Anstey, Leicestershire

Set by Words & Graphics Ltd.
Anstey, Leicestershire
Printed and bound in Great Britain by
T. J. International Ltd., Padstow, Cornwall

1

Jay West, psych-policeman, arrived at headquarters just in time to see a case brought for trial at Ship's Court. As usual Gregson, his chief, was acting as judge and, aside from Kennedy and the communications man, the office was empty. Jay grinned at the operator, nudged his fellow officer to make room on the bench, and nodded towards the sheet of one-way glass separating them from the courtroom.

'What goes on?'

'Waste charge.' Kennedy didn't shift his gaze from the scene. 'Sector four. Know him?'

'No.' Jay looked at the accused, a gardener by his green shorts, still marriageable and with the thin limbs and delicate skin of one who had spent most of his life in the low-gravity upper levels. He was nervous, his eyes wide as he stared at the starkly simple appointments of the court-room; looking at him Jay was reminded of an animal, one of the small, brown, helpless animals of distant Earth. A deer, perhaps? Or was it a rabbit? He couldn't remember, then forgot the problem as Gregson shifted in his chair.

The chief of psych-police was a big, compact man with black eyes matching the gleaming slickness of his uniform. At least twice as old as the accused, he dominated the court by the sheer force of his personality, and as he leaned a little forward over his wide desk, Jay was reminded of yet another animal. A tiger — or was it a cat? He frowned as he tried to recall just when and on what tape he had seen the creatures, and made a mental note to pay more attention to the educational tapes in future. He leaned forward as Gregson's voice came over the speakers.

'Goodwin,' snapped Gregson coldly. '15-3479. Charge of criminal waste. Who accuses?'

'I do, sir.' An older man, also a gardener, shuffled forward, a large plastic bag in his hands. 'My name is Johnson, sir. *14-4562*. I'm head gardener of sector four. I caught young Goodwin here throwing the plant trimmings into the inorganic waste disposal chute. I wouldn't have believed it of him if I hadn't seen it with my own eyes. I'd always liked him and I never guessed that he was like that.' The old man sniffed. 'I've always thought of him like my own son. I — '

'Keep to the point,' snapped Gregson impatiently. 'What happened?'

'I was telling you, sir. We always put all the plant trimmings into the organic waste chute for reclamation. Goodwin here threw them into the wrong chute. If I hadn't seen what he did they'd have been incinerated and we'd have lost everything but the water content.' He glanced at Carter, the other occupant of the room. 'I reported to the officer, sir, and made my charge.'

'I arrested the accused and brought them both here,' said Carter unnecessarily. Gregson nodded.

'Defense?'

'I didn't do it!' The youth licked his lips with nervous defiance as he stared from

Gregson to his accuser. Gregson glanced towards the officer.

'Proof?'

'Here, sir.' Carter took the bag from Johnson, stepped forward and emptied it on the desk. About half a kilogram of brown-edged leaves and dry stalks made a little heap of vegetation on the smooth surface. He stepped back as Gregson looked down at it.

'You found all this?'

'I did.'

'In the inorganic waste chute?'

'Yes.'

'I see,' Gregson leaned back in his chair, the tip of one finger idly stirring the heap of leaves. He didn't speak and aside from the faint rustle of the leaves and the soft, almost imperceptible vibration of the metal walls and floor, so soft and familiar as to be unnoticed, silence filled the court-room.

'Waste,' said Kennedy disgustedly. 'Gregson should send him straight to the converter.'

'You think that he's guilty?' Jay narrowed his eyes as he stared at the pale, sweating face of the accused. Kennedy shrugged.

'What ... ' He broke off as sound came over the speakers.

'I didn't do it,' insisted Goodwin desperately. 'I swear that I didn't do it.'

'How do you account for this vital material being found in the wrong chute?' Gregson's voice was very soft and Jay suddenly remembered what he was reminded of. Not a tiger, but a cat — and the gardener was a mouse. He smiled in quiet pride at his retentive memory. Not bad considering that he had never seen either of the animals except as pictures on a screen. He wanted to tell Kennedy but Goodwin was speaking again so he listened instead.

'I can't account for it, sir. Unless ... '

'Unless what?'

'Johnson's getting to be an old man, sir,' blurted Goodwin. 'He's afraid that I'll take over his job and he's trying to get rid of me.'

'I wouldn't throw vegetation in the inorganic chute,' said Johnson hastily. 'I know how valuable the material is too well for that. I've been a gardener all my life, sir, and I just couldn't do it.' He shook his head in apparent despair. 'It's these youngsters — they just don't stop to think, and if they aren't stopped they'll ruin us with their constant waste.'

'This is a serious charge,' said Gregson heavily; he didn't seem to have heard the counter accusation and defense. 'You know that waste, aside from mutiny, is the most heinous crime there is. Both are punishable by death.' He paused. 'Is there anything you wish to say before I pass sentence?'

'I didn't do it,' repeated Goodwin desperately. 'I'm innocent of the charge.'

'Why doesn't Gregson test him?' said Jay disgustedly. 'Two minutes on the lie detector would clear up the whole thing.' He frowned at Johnson. 'I wouldn't mind betting that the old man's got something to do with this. Look at him, he's as guilty as hell.'

'Better not let Gregson hear you say that,' warned Kennedy. 'He knows what he's doing.'

'Maybe, but I . . . ' Jay broke off as the

communications man called over to him. 'Yes?'

'Call from sector three. That's your sector, isn't it, Jay?'

'That's right.' Jay rose to his feet and crossed over to the operator. 'What's wrong?'

'An accident. Man dead on level nineteen, segment three, cubicle four twenty-seven. Call came from a man named Edwards — he said that he'd wait for you by the booth. Clear it up, will you.'

Jay nodded and, leaving Kennedy still staring at the courtroom, walked out into the Ship.

Jay had never seen an anthill, nor had he ever seen a bee hive, but if he had, then the Ship would have reminded him of both. A huge metal egg, it was honeycombed with concentric levels of cubicles: workshops, recreation rooms, hydroponics farms and yeast culture vats for the production of food; kitchens and mess halls for its preparation and serving. Everything essential to life was contained within the titanic hull, from toys for the new-born to gardens to freshen the air, and the whole incredible mass spun on its central axis, creating an artificial gravity by centrifugal force, a gravity which increased rapidly towards the outer hull and vanished in the central areas.

Men had built it, not on Earth for that would have been impossible, but in space, fashioning it from prefabricated parts hauled by powerful rockets from the planet or brought from the new base at Tycho on the Moon. A mountain of metal had been used in its construction and, when they had finished the shell, they had fitted it with engines powerful enough to illuminate a world, stocked it with seeds and plants, food and fuel, animals and cultures, so that one day the colonists would be able to set up a new Earth beneath an alien sun.

They had planned well, the builders of the Ship. Fired by the discovery of planets circling Pollux, a star only thirty-two light years away, they had determined to smash the barrier between them and interstellar flight. Speed alone couldn't do it. There was still no way to overcome the

Einsteinian equations which set the speed of light as the maximum velocity possible, and at the same time showed that it would take infinite power to reach that velocity. Speed couldn't do it, but time could, and so they had aimed the ship towards Pollux, given it a speed one-tenth that of light, and hoped that the descendants of the original colonists would be able to do what they were unable to do themselves.

But three hundred years is a long time.

First the name of the ship had been discarded from common usage and it had become known only as the Ship. The sense of motion had soon died also, and to the inhabitants of the Ship, the metal cubicles had become their entire universe, static, unchanging, unalterable. They lived and died within the close confines of their metal prison and, with the slow passage of time, even the aim and purpose of their journey became vague and slightly unreal.

But the builders had planned well.

Edwards was fourteenth generation; Jay could tell that without looking at the identification disc on his left wrist. There was a certain stockiness about him, a calm solidity only to be met in the older people. He stepped forward from the booth as he recognized Jay's black shorts and led the officer along a passage.

'He's in here,' he paused by a door. 'I haven't told anyone yet. I called in as soon as I saw what had happened.'

'Were you friends?' Jay didn't enter the room immediately; the passage was deserted and it was as good a place as any for preliminary investigation. 'Did you know him well?'

'Well enough. He worked in yeast and we almost grew up together.' Edwards shook his head. 'I can't understand it. Hans was always a careful sort of man, not the type to mess around with something he knew nothing about. I just can't imagine what made him do it.'

'Do what?'

'You'll see.' Edwards glanced down the long passage narrowing into the distance, both ends curving a little as it followed the circular pattern of the rooms. A young couple came towards them, arm in arm, their heads together, lost in a world of their own. 'Maybe we'd better go inside,' he suggested. 'This passage usually carries a lot of traffic and we don't want a crowd.'

Jay nodded and led the way into the room.

The only two things about the dead man that were recognizable were his yellow shorts and his identification disc. The shorts told Jay that he had worked in the yeast plant: the disc that he was fourteenth generation, his name had been Hans Jensen, and that he had absolutely no right to have done what he apparently had. All electrical gear came under electronics and no one else had the right to remove a masking plate and touch what was behind it. Hans, for some reason, had done just that and had been seared by high voltage current as a result.

Jay dropped to one knee, studying but not touching, his eyes thoughtful as he stared at the evidence. Edwards coughed and shifted his feet.

'What do you make of it?'

'It looks like an accident,' said Jay

carefully. 'He tampered with the connections and got burned for his trouble.' He looked around the room, a normal two-bunk, four-locker sleeping unit. 'Did you share?'

'Yes.'

'Where were you when it happened?'

'Down in the recreation room. Hans and I were watching some tapes when he was called away by some young fellow. I waited for him; then, when he didn't turn up, I guessed that he might have gone to bed. I walked in and found him like this.'

'I see. How long did you wait before following him out of the recreation room?'

'I waited until the end of the tape, about fifteen minutes.'

Edwards hesitated. 'I don't believe that this was an accident.

'What?'

'I said that this was no accident,' repeated Edwards stubbornly. 'I knew Hans too well to ever believe that he would do anything like this. Why should he? He worked in yeast — he wouldn't want to tamper with the electrical gear.

And if he did, he knew enough about high current never to have touched anything.'

'So you think he committed suicide?'

'No. I think that he was murdered.'

Jay sighed and, leaning against the wall, stared at Edwards. Against his shoulder he could feel the slight, never-ending vibrations of voices and music, the susurration of engines and the countless sounds of everyday life, all caught and carried by the eternal metal, all mingling and traveling until damped out by fresher, newer sounds. A philosopher had once called that vibration the life-sound of the Ship; while it could be heard all was well, without it nothing could be right. Jay didn't know about that; all he knew was that he had grown up with the sound, eaten with it, slept with it, lived with it until he was no more consciously aware of it than he was of his own skin.

'So you think that he was murdered,' he said slowly. 'What makes you think that?'

'Simple. Hans would never have removed that plate. And even if he had, he would never have touched a live connection. Hans wasn't a fool.'

'He was an old man,' reminded Jay. 'Old men sometimes do senseless things.'

'Hans wasn't that old. I'll admit he was fourteenth generation, but so what? I'm fifteenth and yet I'm only a couple of years younger than he was. Hans was one of the fittest and most sensible people I've ever known.' Edwards jerked his head in irritation. 'Don't talk to me about age. I know better.'

And that, thought Jay grimly, was the trouble. Generations could be separated by no more than forty years, because every twenty-year period saw an official change in generation number. Hans could have been forty years older than Edwards, but he could also have been one, and Edwards was suspicious.

'Have you anything else, aside from your own knowledge of the dead man, on which to base your statement that he was murdered?' Jay straightened away from the wall as he spoke and stepped toward the burned thing on the floor. Edwards hesitated.

'I'm not sure,' he said slowly. 'What are you getting at?'

'Had he any enemies?'

'Not that I know of. Hans wasn't one to go in for dueling, never had, and he was popular enough in the yeast plant. There's one thing though.'

'Yes?'

'That man I told you about, the youngster who called him away from the recreation room. I know the people in this sector pretty well, and I'd swear to it that he was a stranger and yet . . . ' Edwards broke off, frowning. 'I have the feeling that I know him.'

'Would you be able to recognize him again?'

'Yes, but that isn't what I was going to say. I told you that I waited for a while in the recreation room and then I came up here to bed?'

'You did.'

'Well, as I was walking along the corridor I thought I saw a man leave this room.'

'Are you positive about that?' said Jay sharply. 'You're certain that it was this room?'

15

'No,' admitted Edwards. 'I can't be. You know how it is — they all look alike, and it could have been from the one next to this, or even from one two doors away. I can't swear to it, but I can swear to the fact that the man I saw was the same one who called Hans away from the recreation room'

'And you think that he murdered your friend?'

'What else can I think?' Edwards made a point of not looking down at the charred heap on the floor. 'He called Hans out; I saw him leave this room, or at least I thought that I did. When I arrived here, Hans was dead. If that man had been here with Hans, then why didn't he report the accident — if it was an accident? And why should Hans suddenly leave me, come to this room, take off the masking plate and touch a live connection?' Edwards shook his head. 'None of it makes sense.'

'Of course it doesn't,' said Jay. 'Why should anyone want to kill your friend? The thing is unreasonable. What happened was an accident. We may never know just why Hans wanted to take off the plate, but we can be certain that he never intended to touch the connection. In a way it serves him right for tampering with things outside his department.'

Jay knelt beside the corpse again, then looked up at the sound of a knock on the door. 'Who is it?'

'Conservation squad.'

'Let them in.' Jay rose as two men, both wearing the olive shorts of conservation, entered the room. An electronics man followed them, his bright blue making a dash of color as he stooped over the displayed connections. He grunted as he probed at the wiring, refastened the masking plate, and nodded as he left the room. He didn't look at the dead man. The two olive clad men unfolded a large plastic bag, and, with the ease of long practice, slipped it over what was left of Hans Jensen, slung it over their shoulders, and headed towards the door.

'Where are they taking him?' Edwards looked towards Jay as the door closed behind the grim two and their shapeless burden. Jay shrugged.

'To the converters; you know that.'

'Why there? Aren't you going to perform an autopsy?'

'Why should we?' Jay took a deep breath as he stared at the stubborn expression on the older man's face. 'Cause of death is plain: electrocution by accident. And that is my official finding.'

'It was murder,' insisted Edwards. 'I tell you I knew Hans too well ever to believe that his death was an accident.'

'What proof have you that it was anything but an accident?' demanded Jay. 'You say that you saw a man, you don't know who he is, and you think that he came from this room. You know as well as I do that he could have come from any one of a dozen rooms. You say that you'd recognize him again, and yet you can't be sure that you know him or not. What sort of evidence is that, Edwards? I hate to remind you of this, but you're no longer a young man and it's quite possible that you could have made a mistake.'

'I'm making no mistake,' said Edwards. 'This whole thing looks like a put-up job to me.'

'Are you accusing me of collusion with a murderer?' Jay kept his voice low, but there was something in the way he looked at the yeast worker which caused Edwards to flush and bite his lips. 'Well? Are you?'

'No, of course not!'

'Then you agree with me that Jensen's death was an unfortunate accident?' Jay stared hard at the man. 'It's obvious, isn't it, when you come to think about it?'

'No.' Edwards shook his head, his eyes refusing to meet those of the officer. 'I can't believe that. I knew Hans too well — he would never do a thing like that.'

'You're being stubborn, Edwards,' snapped Jay impatiently. 'I say that it was an accident and that should be good enough. I know how an old man can forget what he's doing, make a stupid mistake, do something to cause his own death. Why don't you leave it at that?'

'I can't.' Edwards looked directly into the blue eyes staring at him. 'Don't ask me why, but I just can't. Hans was my friend! Maybe you wouldn't understand what that means, but I'm not going to ever think that he was fool enough to kill himself.' He clenched his hands. 'I'm going to find that youngster who called him out, the man I'd swear I saw leaving this room. And when I find him, then perhaps we'll learn the truth as to what happened here.'

'I see.' Jay stared at the man, almost pitying him for his obvious sincerity. Then, remembering his duty, he sighed and gripped Edwards by the arm. 'I'm sorry, but you'll have to come with me.'

'Why?' Edwards tried to pull away, then halted, his face whitening from the pain in his arm. 'I've done nothing wrong. Where are you taking me?'

'To headquarters.' Jay released the nerve pressure and led the man towards the door. 'You're a little too certain that Jensen was murdered for my liking. The only way you could be so sure was to have killed him yourself.'

'That's nonsense!' Edwards tried to pull away again, then winced as Jay increased the pressure against the nerve. 'You can't believe that. Hans was my friend — I'd never even think of killing him.'

'Maybe, but I think we'd better let Psycho decide.' Jay didn't look at his prisoner as they walked through the whispering corridors.

2

Kennedy was in the outer office when they arrived. He looked up from the desk, grinned at Jay, then narrowed his eyes at the sight of Edwards.

'Who's this?'

'A prisoner,' said Jay shortly. 'Book and hold him for interrogation. Murder suspect.' He didn't look at the yeast worker. 'Where's Gregson?'

'Inside.' Kennedy jerked his thumb towards the inner office. 'Merrill's with him, though, and I think they want to be alone.' He glared at Edwards. 'Show me your iden.'

Silently Edwards held out his left wrist so that Kennedy could copy his name and number. He stared directly ahead, not showing the least nervousness, and Jay wished that he hadn't had to bring him in. He waited impatiently until Kennedy had booked the details and ordered the man taken to a cell.

'Tell Gregson that I want to see him.'

'Take your time,' said the officer easily. 'I told you that he was busy.' He lounged back in his chair. 'Say, you should have waited to see the end of that waste case. The boy got sent to the converter, that was obvious, but Gregson sure pulled a fast one on the old man.' He chuckled. 'He had him tested by Psycho and found out that he'd been lying his head off.'

'What happened?'

'Converter, of course. What else could happen?'

'And the boy?'

'I told you, the same.' Kennedy chuckled again. 'I told you that Gregson knew what he was doing. He's saved someone a job later on.'

'I don't get it,' said Jay. 'If the boy was innocent, then why eliminate him? I can understand the other one — he was an old man and due anyway. But why the boy?'

'Why ask me?' Kennedy shrugged. 'Maybe he was due, too, and it was the easy way out.' He looked up as the inner door opened and a man came into the outer office. 'Here's Merrill. I guess you can go in now.'

Merrill grinned at Jay as he came towards him and rested a hand familiarly on his shoulder.

'Hi, Jay, how's things?'

'Not so good,' Jay didn't like the smooth, lithe, cat-like man with the pale, almost albino eyes and the too-thin mouth. There was something feral about him, a secret gloating and an almost frightening ruthlessness. Jay had often thought that of them all, Merrill was the only one who really liked his job, that he would have done it without the extra privileges and private rooms which all officers had as a matter of right. He shrugged off the other's hand.

'Going somewhere, Jay?'

'To see Gregson. I'd like you to come with me.'

'Me?' Merrill smiled, showing his perfect white teeth. When he smiled like that he reminded Jay more than ever of a tiger — or was it a weasel? From what he remembered, Jay thought that Merrill combined the worse qualities of both.

'Yes.'

'Is it important, Jay? I'm off duty right now and I've an important date down in sector five.' He smiled again at Jay's expression. 'That's right. With a friend of yours. Susan is getting to be a big girl now.'

'Leave Susan alone,' snapped Jay. 'She's still got a year to go before reaching marriageable status.' He looked pointedly at Merrill's unmarked shorts. 'And you don't intend getting married.'

'So what?' Merrill shrugged. 'We can have fun, can't we? Or are you trying to keep her for yourself?'

'Talk like that, you'll get in trouble with Genetics,' warned Jay. 'You've no business getting too friendly with her, anyway; sector five is my unofficial sector, not yours.'

'It's my official one,' reminded Merrill, 'and I like Susan. I like her a lot.'

'I can't blame you for that,' said Jay tightly. 'but leave her alone. There are plenty of women out of marriageable status available if you want that sort of thing. Run around with the over twenty-fives if you have to, but leave the youngsters alone.' He didn't attempt to disguise his disgust. Respect for the marriage code was indoctrinated into all Ship personnel, and casual relationships with girls of marriageable status or younger were firmly discouraged. You married to have children — or else. After the marriageable status, at twenty-five, you were free to do as you liked, but before that it was strictly hands off. Even through his instinctive anger he knew that Merrill was deliberately goading him. If the man ever tried to go against the code, he would be eliminated, and Jay vaguely hoped that if such a thing ever happened he would be the one to get the job.

'Forget it!' Merrill smiled again, this time without humor. 'I was only kidding.'

'Were you?' Jay shook his head. 'Funny, I must be totally devoid of a sense of humor. Somehow I don't find immorality the slightest bit amusing.' He stepped towards the inner office. 'Well? Are you coming?'

'Must I?' Merrill hesitated, his pale eyes watchful. 'What do you want me in there for?'

'Come in and find out,' snapped Jay, opening the door and stepping into the inner office.

As usual, Gregson was alone. He sat at his desk radiating a subtle power and machine-like efficiency. He didn't speak as Jay entered, but his black eyes were thoughtful as he saw Merrill, and he looked at Jay, waiting for him to speak.

'I've got a man outside,' Jay said curtly. 'Edwards, a yeast worker. I had to bring him in.'

'Why?'

'He suspects too much.' Jay looked at Merrill. 'You did a lousy job,' he said bitterly. 'Why don't you use your imagination a little more and your mouth a little less.'

'What!' Merrill seemed to recoil into himself and his pale eyes glittered with anger. 'I'll call you out for that. Damn you, West, you can't talk that way and get away with it. Name the time!'

'There'll be no dueling between officers,' said Gregson coldly. 'Any further such talk and I'll have you both in front of Psycho.' He looked at Jay. 'Report.'

'I was called to a case on level nineteen, room 427, sector three.' He stared at Merrill. 'Your sector.'

'Keep to the point,' snapped Gregson. 'Well?'

'A man, Hans Jensen, had apparently died from accidental touching of electrical circuits.' Jay shrugged. 'That, in itself, was bad enough. A yeast worker messing around with electronics — the thing is incredible! But Merrill's blundering made it even worse.'

'Did it?' said Merrill tightly. 'How?'

'You were seen. Edwards, the man I brought in, swears that he would know you again.'

'That isn't true!' Merrill turned to Gregson. 'I did a neat, quick job, and West can't say otherwise. I — '

'Be silent!' Gregson didn't raise his voice, but the officer choked and bit off what he was going to say. The chief nodded to Jay. 'Start from the beginning.'

'I found Jensen crouched over a removed masking plate. He was charred almost to a crisp; death, of course, was instantaneous He shared a four-unit room with Edwards, his friend, and they seemed to have been pretty close. Edwards refuses to believe that the death was accidental. He stated that it was murder. I tried to talk him out of it, but he insisted that Jensen just wouldn't have done what he was supposed to have done. Frankly, I don't blame him. The thing was so amateur that it leaves little doubt. If I hadn't known better, I would never have believed that it was Merrill's work.'

'I see.' Gregson stared at Merrill. 'Well?'

'I did the best I could,' said Merrill sullenly. 'Jensen was awkward. I'd tried to call him out a couple of times before, but he avoided dueling. I couldn't get him alone and it was only because I told him that someone was waiting for him that he agreed to come with me at all.'

'Why?' snapped Gregson sharply. 'Did he suspect you?'

'I don't think so. He couldn't have, or he never would have allowed himself to be alone with me.' Merrill gulped as he saw Gregson's expression. 'It's easy enough for West to talk, but he didn't have to do the job. I tell you the man was suspicious, not of me, but of things in general. A lot of these old timers are — they seem to sense that something's going to happen to them.'

'Stop excusing yourself,' said Gregson coldly. 'What happened?'

'I managed to get him to take me to his room. I had to work fast — I guessed that his friend would be looking for him soon — so I knocked him out, tore off the masking plate, and let his hand fall on a live connection. Even at that I had little time. I saw someone coming down the corridor as I left the room.'

'That was Edwards,' said Jay grimly. 'I told you that he had seen you.'

'Well, what of it?' said Merrill defiantly. 'He can't prove anything.'

'Prove anything!' Gregson half-rose from his chair, his eyes hard with cold fury. 'You fool! Haven't you eliminated enough people to learn by now that suspicion of what we are doing is the very thing we must avoid? If this man, this Edwards, is suspicious, then he doesn't need proof! His suspicions are dangerous

30

enough. He will talk, compare notes with others, spread rumors and, before we know it, the whole Ship will guess what is going on.' He sank back into the chair. 'You say that you brought him in, West?'

'Yes, Kennedy booked him and put him into a cell. Suspicion of murder,' Jay shrugged. 'He's innocent, of course, but what else could I do?'

'Nothing. At least you acted as though you had brains and intelligence. I wish that I could say the same about someone else.'

'If you mean me, Gregson, then why don't you say so?' Merrill stepped forward, his pale eyes and thin lips betraying his anger. 'I killed Jensen, didn't I? What more do you want?'

'You eliminated Jensen,' corrected Gregson coldly. 'And I expect a little more than a bungled, amateur job from any of my officers, including you.'

'Bungled?'

'Yes. West is right in what he says. No yeast worker would dare to tamper with electrical installations; that was your first mistake. The other was in allowing yourself to be seen in a compromising position. You have committed the stupidest mistake of all — you have a witness to what you did.'

'That was bad luck.'

'No, there is no such thing as luck in what we have to do. Either you can do your job as it should be done, or you are unfit to hold your position.' Gregson leaned a little forward, his voice falling to a feral purr. 'You know what that means, I take it?'

Merrill did. Jay did. Everyone connected with psych-police did: the officers, the Psycho operator, the rarely seen, almost unknown hierarchy of the Ship. They knew it if no one else did, and it was that knowledge which had to be kept from the people.

Unfit Personnel, Disposal Of: para 1927 of the Ship's Code. Unfit meaning any and everyone who was not wholly capable of doing their job: the ill; the diseased; the barren; the infertile; the neurotic; those that ate too much, who had slow reflexes, who were physically below par, who were mentally unstable.

The unnecessary, the unessential, the old. Especially the old.

For someone had to make room for the new generations.

'I . . . ' Merrill swallowed, sweat glistening on his naked torso. 'You wouldn't eliminate me.'

'Why not?' Gregson curved the corners of his mouth in a humorless smile. 'Never make that mistake, Merrill. I'll admit that it isn't easy to select replacements, men who can be trusted to hold the knowledge you have, to turn themselves into merciless eliminators for the common good. But we can do it. We found you and we could find someone to replace you.' Again he gave a thin mockery of a smile. 'We will have to eventually, so why not now?'

'You . . . ' Merrill seemed to shake himself and suddenly he was calm. 'All right then. So you're going to kill me.' He bared his teeth and flexed his hands. 'Let me see you try.'

'You'd fight, of course,' said Gregson calmly, 'but even with your advantage you still couldn't win.' He looked at Jay.

'Would you care to take the assignment?'

'Now?'

'No, not now. Not while he is on his guard and expecting an attack. Later, when he has almost forgotten his danger, when he is asleep, perhaps, or watching an educational tape. Could you do it then?'

'Yes.'

'You see?' Gregson looked at Merrill, something like contempt showing in his eyes. 'You have a strong survival instinct — you need it to be what you are — but we'd get you in the end. No man can stay alert forever, and you'd never be quite sure when it was safe to relax. You have to sleep, you know. Even if you hid out in No-Weight, you'd still have to sleep sometimes. And where would you eat? You'd have to eat, you know, Merrill. And you could never be wholly certain that your food hadn't been tampered with, could you?' He relaxed and smiled at the discomforted officer. 'If Psycho decided that you were unfit and had to be eliminated, then we could do it. You wouldn't be the first officer to meet with an unfortunate 'accident' and you wouldn't be the last. We all get our turn.'

'Do we?' Merrill shrugged and stared at Jay. 'Well? Do you want to try now, or wait until later?'

Jay hesitated, wondering just what was in Gregson's mind. The threat was an empty one, he knew that: no victim was ever warned that he was due for elimination; to do so would be to destroy the very secrecy they had sworn to maintain. Merrill was safe, and, knowing the man as he did, Jay knew that he knew it. There were other, deeper reasons for this by-play, and Jay had an uneasy feeling that he knew what they were.

It was never easy to eliminate an officer. For one thing, each man knew his fellow operators, and for another, each had been trained to the ultimate in unarmed combat. Working as they did and being what they were, a sense of comradeship was inevitable. Any group of men sharing a common secret, armed with the knowledge of hidden power, had to have an affinity towards each other; there could always come a time when one man on an assignment would spare his ex-fellow officer.

Unless he had a personal hate against his victim.

Merrill hated Jay, now more than ever, and Jay knew it. He also disliked Merrill and would cheerfully accept the assignment of eliminating him. Was Gregson's entire purpose to forge himself a weapon, one against the other? Jay didn't know but, looking at the hard eyes and ruthless features of the chief, he felt that he had made a pretty shrewd guess. He looked at Merrill.

'I can't answer that until I receive an assignment card,' he said coldly. 'Don't you think this foolishness has gone far enough?'

'Has it?' Merrill looked at Gregson. 'Well?'

'West is right,' said Gregson calmly. 'I only wanted to show you how futile it is for you to get delusions of grandeur — and how easy it is to prick the bubble. You were careless, Merrill. It is the first time, I admit, but the question now is what are we going to do about it?' He looked at Jay 'Any suggestions?'

'We can confront Merrill with Edwards. If the man recognizes him, we can put Merrill to the test and prove his guilt. Edwards will be satisfied with 'justice' and Merrill can go to the converters.' Jay smiled at Merrill's instinctive gesture.

'That is one way,' agreed Gregson quietly. 'We would lose an officer for the sake of a principle, but it might be worth it to kill incipient rumors. Is that your only suggestion?'

'No. The obvious way out of the difficulty is to eliminate Edwards. That was why I brought him in under arrest. No matter what happens now the man will talk, if for no other reason than to prove himself smarter than the officer who investigated the case. Me.' Jay shrugged at Gregson's expression.

'Edwards is an old man, almost forty. He has no friends now that Jensen is dead. He will hardly be missed and soon forgotten. He would be due for elimination soon anyway, so we aren't really going against the code. I can mention to one or two people in the yeast plant where he worked that Edwards killed his friend in a fit of temporary insanity and has been taken away for treatment. They will believe me — no reason for them to do otherwise — and we will have been saved a job for later on.'

'Good,' said Gregson, and Jay knew that he was applauding the prospect of a 'job' saved rather than anything else. Too many incidents would lead to an ingrained distrust and suspicion of the psych-police — the very thing which they wanted to avoid. Such suspicion would make further eliminations even more difficult and in time, would lead to open revolt and the dread specter of mutiny.

'Shall I tell Kennedy to send Edwards to the converters then?' Jay didn't look at Merrill as he spoke and felt annoyed himself for feeling a sense of shame. Gregson nodded.

'Do that. I'll report to Psycho that he has been eliminated and have his card expelled.' He rose and jerked his head in dismissal. 'You've done a good job, West. Merrill, you're off duty I believe. Get out of here and count yourself lucky. But remember this, there won't be a second time. Any more bungling and I'll be looking for a replacement officer. Now get out!'

They didn't speak as they left and Jay was glad of it. He could almost feel the radiated hatred from the pale-eyed man and found difficulty in controlling his own dislike. Silently he watched Merrill stride arrogantly from the office, his sandals slapping against the metal flooring as he thrust his way into the corridor. Then, because he was still on stand-by duty, Jay sat down before one of the screens and pressed the activating button.

The educational tape was one of old-time court procedure as practiced on Earth at the time the Ship had left on its long voyage to Pollux over three centuries ago.

Jay found it faintly amusing.

3

Sam Aldway worked in hydroponics and hated every minute of it. He scowled at the ranked vats of nutrient solutions, at the glossy richness of the healthy root-crops he was tending, and savagely pruned any leaf which showed the least hint of browning or of not doing its proper job.

'Take it easy, Sam,' snapped his overseer. 'Cut back too far and you'll do more harm than good.'

'I know what I'm doing,' said Aldway sullenly. He snipped off another leaf. 'Did you put in my transfer?'

'To the psych-police?' The overseer laughed. 'Get wise to yourself, Sam. They won't take you now. You're too old for one thing, and for another, your work is here.'

'I asked you if you'd put in my transfer.'

'I heard you. The answer is no. I didn't

put it in because I know that it's a waste of time.'

'I thought so.' Sam dropped his shears and stood, legs straddled, glaring at the older man. 'I've a damn good mind to call you out for that. You put in that request now or you and I will have a date together down in the stadium.'

'You can't make me duel,' said the overseer uncomfortably. 'I don't have to fight you.'

'You're not married, are you?' Sam glared at the other's unmarked brown shorts. 'You're of dueling age, and, if I say so, then you've got to meet me.'

'No I haven't,' said the overseer quickly, 'I can always refer it to the P.P.'

'You think that the psych-police will help you?' Sam deliberately spat on the floor next to the overseer's sandals. 'Why should they want to protect a coward?' He prodded at the overseer's chest with his stiffened forefinger. 'You put in that request for transfer now, understand? Now!'

The older man swallowed, hesitated a moment, then nodded and walked away.

He was sweating as he moved to the phone to put in the request. Aldway had the reputation of being a dangerous man; he was still smarting at the blow to his pride at losing his wife who, when he had reached twenty-five and had changed his white-banded shorts for the unmarked ones he would wear for the rest of his life, had shown him the door to their family unit. Protest had been useless, the code was rigidly enforced, and so he had gone into bachelor quarters, sharing with an unsympathetic listener and trying, without much success, to enter into an agreement with one of the available women.

He had taken his revenge against the system by dueling.

The overseer lifted the receiver, punched a number, and listened until a voice spoke from the other end.

'P.P. Headquarters.'

'Overseer Brenson, 14-9741, sector five. I've got a young man here who — '

'Wait a minute. Are you reporting an accident?'

'Hold on then. I'll put you through to

the officer in charge of your section.' There was a click, a buzz and then a fresh voice. 'Merrill here. Officer in charge of sector five. What's your trouble?'

'A case of dissatisfaction in hydroponics farm eighteen, sir.' Benson looked across to where Sam lounged, apparently working, but obviously listening to the conversation. 'Name: Sam Aldway. Cause: wants transfer to P.P. I've tried to tell him that his request won't be entertained, but he won't listen and insists that I put it through.'

'Which generation?'

'Fourteenth, but he's just out of marriageable status.'

'Too old,' said Merrill decisively. 'Tell him that he's wasting his time.'

'I've done that, sir.'

'Then why bother me? You're his boss, aren't you?'

'I'm supposed to be,' said Brenson bitterly, 'but he's a cocky young devil and threatens to call me out.' He hesitated, looking at Sam. 'Could you have a word with him?'

'No,' snapped Merrill. 'Handle it yourself.'

'I can't,' wailed Brenson. 'He's dangerous, I tell you! He's killed at least three men already and I don't want to be the fourth.'

'Afraid of a duel?' The transmitted voice held a sneer. Brenson gulped.

'Yes,' he admitted. 'At least I am with him. I wouldn't stand a chance. He's vicious and fights to the death.'

'Is that so?' Merrill sounded thoughtful. 'A born killer, eh?'

'That's the way it seems,' admitted Brenson. 'I've never met anyone else like him.'

'I see.' The phone hummed silently for a moment. 'Tell you what I'll do. I'll have a talk with him and see if I can't straighten this thing out. Where will he be after duty?'

Brenson cupped his hand over the mouthpiece and yelled to Sam. 'Where will you be after duty?'

'Why?' Sam came closer. 'Who wants to know?'

'Merrill, the P.P. officer. Well?'

'Down in the Gyms, the same place I always go.' Sam came even closer as

Brenson removed his hand and spoke into the phone. 'What's he want me for?'

'He'll be down in the gymnasium,' said Brenson to Merrill.

'Right. I'll probably meet him there. Tell him to expect me.'

'Thank you, sir,' said Brenson fervently. 'Thank you!' But he was speaking into a dead phone.

The gymnasiums were down on the lowest level, together with the maternity wards and kindergartens, the waste reclamation units and recreation rooms. Here, though Sam didn't know it, gravity was twice Earth normal, ideal conditions both for exercise and the rearing of a strong and virile population. To survive at all, the babies had to be strong and with the passing of more than three hundred years the weak and frail-boned had long ago been weeded out.

Sam spent a lot of time in the exercise rooms. He was proud of his smooth, lithemuscled body, far more efficient than the classical type with its great masses of knotted muscle, its tendency to fat and its high oxygen and nutriment requirements.

Ship personnel were all of a slim, graceful, long-muscled type with perfect control and unsuspected strength, the ideal pattern of Man as arrived at by Genetics and the necessity of achieving maximum efficiency with minimum food requirement.

As usual, he started on the punch-bag, driving slamming blows against the plastic to tune up his arms and shoulders. From there he stayed awhile on the pedal-press, thrusting his legs against high-tension springs to develop his thighs, calves and loins. Weights next, and the routine drill for stomach and back.

He was busy at shadow-boxing when he became aware of a pale-eyed man, wearing the black shorts of the psych-police, staring at him.

'Merrill?'

Merrill nodded, staring hard at the young man. 'So you're Aldway, the terror of hydroponics,' he said, and Sam flushed at the hint of a sneer in the cold voice. 'What's the matter, Sam, can't you find anyone better to fight with than old men?'

'Did Brenson tell you that?' Sam lashed

out at the punch bag, twisting his fist at the moment of impact and baring his teeth as the heavy, sand-filled container swung away from him. Merrill shook his head.

'Brenson told me nothing I didn't already know.' He steadied the bag. 'I've heard that you fancy yourself as a duelist. Is that right?'

'Could be.' Sam punched the bag again, seeming to take a vicarious satisfaction in punishing the unfeeling plastic. 'Why?'

'How many men have you called out?'

'Five.'

'How many wins?'

'Five. Three dead, the other two were first-time duels.' Despite his air of indifference, Sam couldn't restrain his pride; unconsciously his eyes dropped to the five red spots on the inside of his left arm. Merrill didn't seem impressed.

'Bare hands or weapons?'

'Two with knives, the other three bare-handed.' Sam sounded apologetic. 'Two of the bare-handed combats were first-timers and the ref stopped the bout before I could finish.' He stared at Merrill. 'Why all the questions? I haven't broken the code.'

'Did I say you had?' Merrill looked around the crowded exercise room. 'I hear that you want to join the P.P.'

'That's right.' Sam looked hopefully at the officer. 'Can you get me in? I'm a good man and I'd make a good officer. I — '

'You're too old,' said Merrill flatly, and smiled at the other's expression. 'Ten years ago you might have stood a chance, but not now. You must be at least thirty.'

'Twenty-seven.'

'That's what I said, you're ten years too late. You've been married and had your kids; now you can look forward to a nice tranquil old age in bachelor quarters, tending your plants and filling your educational quota.' Merrill smiled again at Aldway's expression of disgust. 'Or you can keep calling men out until you find one a little better than yourself, in which case you needn't worry about old age — you won't have any.'

'Is that bad?' Sam hit the punch bag as

though he were punishing the entire Ship system. 'This is a hell of a life anyway.'

'Maybe we could do something about it?' suggested Merrill softly. He took hold of Sam's arm. 'First, let's eat. I'm hungry.'

As an officer Merrill was entitled to eat in any mess he happened to choose, but Sam had to go to his sector's mess and show his identity disc. The meal, as usual, was hydroponic vegetables with yeast as the staple, well-disguised and with a choice of three main dishes. Merrill chose lemon sole, Aldway fillet of steak, neither fancying the roast chicken. The food was the same, different only in shape and flavor, but the dietitians had long known that variety was essential for good health and appetite. Both men ate as fit men should eat, with hungry zest and applied concentration. Merrill finished the last of his sweet, synthetic ice cream — small in bulk but rich in protein and carbohydrates — and sat back, toying with his ration of brackish water and waiting for his companion to finish his meal.

'Lousy food,' Sam commented, wiping

his mouth on the back of his hand. 'No fresh fruits — and we grow any amount of them in hydroponics. Where do they all go to, that's what I'd like to know?'

Merrill could have told him where they went, where Sam knew they went had he but exercised his memory. To the very young, the nursing and expectant mothers, to the growing generations who needed the fresh, natural vitamins more than did the adult population. He didn't bother to explain.

'You said something,' reminded Sam hopefully. He swallowed his water ration and tossed the plastic cup into the disposal basket. 'Did you mean it?'

'That depends.' Merrill sipped his own water, his eyes watchful over the rim of the cup. 'How badly do you want to break out of the rut?'

'Bad enough to do anything,' said Sam tensely. 'Waste! If I don't do something soon I'll go crazy and be carried off for treatment.' He stared at Merrill. 'Look, I don't care what I do. I'll do anything you want me to, just so long as you get me away from that damn farm. I'll work in No-Weight, I'll give you half my rations — anything. You name it, I'll do it. I mean it, Merrill. Anything!'

'I think you do,' said Merrill quietly, and his pale eyes were thoughtful as he examined the man at his side. Though Sam didn't know it, he had literally signed his own death warrant. The Ship could not tolerate any unbalanced individual and, if Merrill reported the conversation as he should do, Sam would be eliminated. Even his dueling propensities, while of value in helping to keep down the older section of the population, meant little against the potential danger of his neurosis. Such a man was fully capable of hitting back in many ways against a system he imagined had hurt him. He could deliberately waste essential material, ruin an entire crop by carelessness, spread alarm and despondency by whispered rumors or, as he was already doing, cause unrest and fear by his arrogance.

Sam had to die.

But how and when he died was something else.

Merrill finished his water, threw the cup into the basket and rose to his feet. Sam rose with him, his eyes asking questions, but it wasn't until they were outside the mess that Merrill spoke.

'You want to join the psych-police, right?'

'Yes.'

'Well, you can't and you may as well know it.' Merrill was deliberately blunt. 'That is you can never become a uniformed member of the P.P., but . . . .' He let his voice fade into silence, waiting for the fish to gulp the bait.

'Any job will do,' pleaded Aldway. 'I don't care about the uniform.' He lied and Merrill knew it. 'Can't I be your assistant, or something?'

And there it was. The driving complex which demanded authority, no matter how little or how disguised. The crying need for power at any price, the desire to swagger and rule, to be dominant and boastful. Merrill had no delusions as to what would happen if he made Sam his assistant. At first the man might live up to his promises; then, inevitably, he would need to show off, to display his powers to advertise his arrogance. Not if he lived to Journey's End, would he ever learn how to use authority but Merrill knew that Sam wouldn't live anywhere near that long.

He pretended to consider the suggestion, hooding his eyes as if he were deep in thought. Finally he nodded as if coming to a decision.

'You'll take me!' Sam looked as though he could kiss the metal at their feet. 'You'll give me a job away from the farm?'

'Not so fast. I've already got an assistant and I can't have two.' Merrill almost smiled at Sam's expression. 'You'll have to wait until I can get rid of him.'

'Oh.' Sam gulped, his rosy dreams vanishing as soon as they had come. 'How long will that be?'

'Who knows? I don't like the man, but I can hardly call him out — dueling isn't allowed for officers — and no one else is likely to do it.' Merrill paused, waiting for Sam to make the obvious offer. 'No, Sam, I don't think that you're good enough.'

'You don't think so?' Sam flexed his

muscles. 'I'm fit and I'm trained. I can snap a man's neck like a stick and I know all the holds.' He held out his left arm. 'You think I collected these by imagination? Show me who it is and let me at him.'

'He's not a dueling man, Sam. It'll be a first bout and the ref will stop any killing.'

'If he gets the chance. I've learned a trick or two since I started and I can move faster than any damn ref.' Sam gripped Merrill's arm. 'Just show me who it is, boss, that's all I ask. Just give me the chance to get him out of the way.'

'You think that you could do it?' Merrill hesitated as though in doubt. 'He's pretty well trained and you might not find it easy — he could kill you, you know. It wouldn't be your first time in the stadium, and if you killed him you'd have to make it look like a real accident. You sure that you could do it?'

'Give me the chance,' repeated Sam. 'That's all I ask.'

'Right, but there's something I'm going to do before you call him out.' Merrill smiled into the wondering face of his dupe. 'I'm going to take you to the exercise rooms and we're going to have a fight.'

'Fight?' Sam stepped back, his eyes reflecting his bewilderment. 'Why?'

Merrill didn't answer; he was already leading the way towards the lowest level.

4

George Curtway looked up at a knock on the door, leaned forward to switch off the view, and straightened just in time to be kissed by a raven-haired young woman.

'Susan!' He smiled at his daughter as she settled herself in a chair. 'You're early.'

'We got all the young devils topped and tailed and settled down, and Matron said that I could end-shifts early as we'd all worked so hard.' Susan paused to draw a deep breath. 'My! I must be getting old. I hardly ran at all on the way up.' She looked towards the viewer. 'What's showing?'

'Some old tapes from Earth. Animals and farming scenes.'

'Young animals?'

'Don't you get enough young animals working in maternity?' He smiled with parental pride at her neat figure in the form-fitting pink halter and shorts. She made a face and leaned forward to switch on the screen.

'Babies aren't animals.'

'What else are they?' He didn't look at the screen as it flared to life with the transmitted images from central control. 'A baby is as much an animal as . . . ' he glanced at the screen, 'as that young goat there, or is it a lamb?'

'No idea.' She smiled at him. 'Anyway, babies are far more interesting than a lot of silly old animals we'll probably never even see.'

'We will one day, Susan. When the Ship reaches Journey's End, we'll have to know all about animals and everything else.'

'Perhaps, but until then I'll worry about babies.' She looked at the images for a moment then, her youthful exuberance overcoming her patience, interrupted her father's viewing again. 'Fred's not here yet?'

'Can you see him?' George stared around the stark simplicity of the tiny room. Susan flushed.

'Sorry, that was a stupid remark.' She

hesitated. 'Have you seen anything of Jay lately?'

'No.' Something in George's voice made her look at him. George didn't return her look; he sat, staring at the pictured scene, his mouth set with unusual firmness.

'What's the matter, Dad? Don't you like Jay?'

'Jay's okay, but don't get too involved with him, Susan.'

'Why not?' She leaned forward and switched off the viewer. 'That's better, now you can answer me. What's wrong with Jay?'

'Nothing.' He reached for the switch and she caught his hand. 'What you are trying to do, girl?' he said with mock severity. 'If I don't fill my educational quota I'll be downgraded and lose the privilege of having a single room. Would you like to visit me in a common recreational chamber?'

'They won't downgrade you, and you must have seen those tapes so often that you know them by heart.' She moved so that she sat in front of the screen. 'Now,

58

answer me. What is wrong with Jay?'

'Nothing.'

'Yes there is or you wouldn't look like that.' She became serious. 'I want an answer, dad.'

'Jay's fifteenth generation,' he said reluctantly. 'You're sixteenth and almost of marriageable status. You know that you can't marry Jay.'

'Why not?'

'Because he's too old for one thing and Genetics would never allow it for another. Now are you satisfied?'

'No. Jay's a young man and I can't see anything to stop us getting married.'

'Then you're either a fool or you're just plain stubborn — and I know that you're not a fool.' George smiled at his daughter. 'Just supposing that you were allowed to marry Jay. He's about twenty-one or twenty-two and you're only seventeen. By the time you're ready for marriage he'll be a year older. That means that he's only got two or three years of marriageable status while you'll have seven. That's not even long enough for you to have your two children and certainly not long enough for you to be together in family quarters.' He touched her hair, letting his hand caress her short curls. 'After you're twenty-five you can do as you like, but until then you'll have to let Genetics decide. After all, you want children, don't you?'

She didn't blush — there was no such thing as false modesty in the Ship — but he read his answer in her eyes. Every female on board wanted children, as many as possible, and as soon as they had reached optimum childbearing age, Susan was no different from any other woman of her age group, and her decision to work in maternity showed that she was normally healthy and had a strong survival instinct. Though she didn't know it, the betting was high in her favor among her overseers that she would be allowed to have more than the usual two children.

She looked up as the door opened and Fred, her brother, came towards them. Fred was twenty and still proud of his white-banded shorts. He looked at Susan and smiled with the superior knowledge of a two-year married man.

'Hi, youngster. Dried your ears yet?'

He ducked as she swung at him, a little clumsy at having come down from the lowgravity levels and not having had time to become accustomed to the Earth normal on the twentieth level. George watched them for a while; then, reaching out, he slapped Susan's rear and pulled her away.

'Give him a rest, Susan. He's an old married man now and not what he used to be.'

They all laughed.

'Had a hard one this shift,' said Fred, sitting next to his sister on the narrow bench. 'Water condensed in a conduit and caused a short. Some of the fans went out and the air wasn't circulating.' He chuckled. 'You should have heard those gardeners! To hear them talk you'd think that they ran the Ship.' Like his father Fred was in electronics.

'They do in a way, you know,' said George quietly. 'If it wasn't for the gardens we'd have no fresh air. Any idea what caused the short?'

'I told you, water condensed in a conduit.'

'Yes, but how? Those conduits are supposed to be waterproof and anyway, even if water did permeate, it shouldn't have caused a blow-out.'

'That's true,' said Fred thoughtfully. 'It shouldn't, should it?'

'Was the insulation bad? Damaged in any way? Frayed or worn?' George frowned at his son's hesitation. 'Come on, son. It isn't enough just to repair the fault; you've got to find out what caused it in the first place and make sure that it doesn't happen again.'

'I know that,' snapped Fred testily. 'You don't have to teach me primary electronics. It's just that I've never thought of the Ship being at fault at all.'

'It's at fault all right,' said George grimly. 'I've found that out in my own work often enough. Cracked insulation and corroded metal. Warped conduits and crystallized unions. Intermittent shorts and erratic current flow. Naturally,' he said bitterly, 'the atomic engineers won't admit that their piles are at fault. No, it's always our equipment — and yet I know for a fact that their generators are falling in efficiency. Why even Psy — ' He broke off, biting his lips.

'What's that, dad?' Fred leaned forward, curiosity large on his expressive features. 'You said something about Psycho?'

'No I didn't.'

'You started to. What was it?'

'Nothing. Forget it.'

'But I want to know, dad,' insisted Fred. 'Maybe I'll be able to service the admin equipment one day and anything you can tell me now will help my promotion later on. What was it you were saying about Psycho?'

'I told you to forget it,' snapped George sharply. 'Remember your manners and decent behavior. Unwanted curiosity is as bad as a violation of declared privacy.' He glared at his son for a moment, then he relaxed as Susan touched his hand. 'What is it?'

'Why should you be having all this trouble with the electronic equipment?' she asked with a woman's instinctive knowledge of when to change the subject. 'Was it always as bad as this?'

'I can't see how it could have been,' said George. 'Even the educational tapes are showing signs of wear; some of them are quite blurred, and others that I remember don't seem to be shown at all now.'

'And are there more shorts and things?'

'Yes, but we can expect that. The Ship is old; you're the sixteenth generation to be born in it, and that is a long time. Things wear, Susan, and grow old just like people do. Insulation dries out and cracks, moisture condenses in those cracks and corrodes the metal. Deposits build and the alloys transmute a little. Capacities vary, resistances alter a trifle, cables can't carry such a big load as they used to.' George shrugged. 'It all adds up to a great big headache for the electricians.'

'Does age do all that?' Susan looked scared. 'If that's happening now, then what about later? We're still a long way from Journey's End, aren't we?'

'I suppose so,' said George, 'but it isn't

only age that's the trouble.' He rested his hand against the wall. 'Here, put your hand close to mine. Feel it?'

'Feel what?' Susan frowned as she tried to concentrate. 'It just feels like a normal wall to me.'

'Forget the metal. Imagine that you're listening with your finger tips instead of your ears. Now do you feel it?'

'No, I . . . ' Susan laughed. 'Now I see what you mean. The vibration. But it's been there all the time — it's always been there.'

'Yes,' said George quietly. 'Every atom of the Ship is vibrating and has done for a long time now. Those vibrations are part of the trouble. Metal tends to crystallize when vibrated for too long and the harmonics can play waste with the insulation.' He shrugged. 'Nothing we can do about it, of course, but I thought that Fred might like to know.' He stretched, his well-kept muscles rippling beneath his satin skin. 'Well, children, anything else an old man could tell you?'

'You're not old,' protested Susan. 'You're only fourteenth generation after all.' She began to count on her fingers. 'Let me see now. I'm seventeen and sixteenth, so you must be — '

'Anything between fifty-seven and thirty-seven.' George shrugged. 'I'm thirty-nine if you must know, and there aren't many men my age still working.' He grinned at his son. 'I attribute old age to a firm resolve never to duel. A resolution I suggest you strictly follow, both of you. Personally, I've never seen the sense in two, apparently normal people, battering or cutting each other to death for the sake of an imagined insult.'

'Suppose someone calls you a waster,' suggested Fred. 'Sure you wouldn't stand an insult like that without doing something about it?'

'Look, son,' said George seriously. 'Never mind what they call you. If a man is low enough to accuse you of waste, call in the psych-police and ask him to prove it. No one has to stand that kind of language but there are other ways of settling it without risking your neck.' He looked at his daughter. 'That goes for you too, Susan. You're not in any danger now, either of you, but later you may be. I've seen quite innocent people fall victims to some puffed-up bully with a knack of getting under the skin, and women can be the worst offenders when they think a pretty, newly-available woman is cutting in on their boyfriends. Stay well away from it, and let the fools fight. There's no conservation in getting yourself killed for a public show.'

'You talk like an old man giving his children some final advice,' laughed Susan. 'We'll depend on you to keep us out of trouble.'

'Don't do that,' said George seriously. 'Never rely on anyone but yourselves.'

'Not even the psych-police?' Fred looked knowingly at Susan. 'The officer can be very helpful at times.'

'Why?' George stared at his daughter's flushed face. 'Has Merrill been bothering you again?'

'No, dad. Fred's only joking.' She glared at her brother and signaled to him to keep quiet. 'He's dropped by maternity a time or two, and we may have eaten together, but there's nothing in it. Merrill isn't marriageable, no P.P. officer is — you know that.'

'Maybe not, but I don't trust that man and I'd rather you didn't see him.' George shook his head as if dismissing an unpleasant subject. 'Looks as if Jay won't be coming this time.' He looked at Susan again. 'Maybe it's just as well.'

'Jay isn't bad,' defended Fred. 'I like him, even though I wouldn't like his job. Must be rotten for him to have to keep crawling through the ventilation shafts.' He smiled down at his own blue shorts. 'I'm glad I'm not in ventilation. Give me electronics every time!'

'If you didn't like it you wouldn't be doing it,' reminded George. He leaned forward and switched on the viewer. 'Let's see what's on.'

The screen blurred then steadied into a schematic of dismantled wiring and tiny transistors. Together with the diagram, a smoothly modulated voice coupled with lines of running text explained what each piece was, how it operated, its purpose and the methods of construction and repair. George leaned forward with

professional interest, but Fred grunted
with disgust.

'Waste! Who wants homework? Let's
find some entertainment.'

He reached forward for the change
switch.

5

The dream was always the same. He was dead and they had taken him to the converter. The grim men in olive had collected him in their plastic bag and delivered him at the place where the last indignities would be carried out with cold, scientific detachment. They would render him down. They would extract the last droplet of moisture from his blood and body, grind his bones to fertilizer, process his flesh and tissue, his skin, his internal organs. Medical students would cut and probe as they learned their trade, and when they had finished, his outraged body would be used down to the last scraping of protoplasm.

On the Ship there could be no waste and they would return him to the dust and chemicals from which he had sprung. They would reclaim everything he had used other than the energy he had needed and expended to stay alive. All of him.

Every last, tiny fragment that had walked and talked, hoped and planned, loved and dreamed. All except the still unknown, wholly intangible mesh of electricity which made him peculiarly different from all others. The ego, the essential 'I was,' the one thing the surgeons and the butchers could never hope to save.

And with its loss he would be as though he had never existed.

Gregson muttered as he turned and when he awoke his face and torso were damp with sweat. He lay for a while, staring into the soft darkness of his room, sensing rather than actually feeling the susurration of trapped sound that was the life noise of the Ship. He liked the darkness. There was too little of it and, only when he had closed himself in, could he switch off the lights and sit and think and plan and dream. There were no polished bulkheads in the dark, no mirrors, no wondering expressions and doubtful eyes. No men to stare and women to question. No passing of time or hate or envy or fear.

As usual at such times, he sought

escape from the present into the past, letting his memory scuttle down the years back to the time when he was very young and life was something that would go on forever. His childhood was spent in a family unit with parents who remained together because of the code and not through love. He had left them, as all children left their parents, when he was twelve. Long before that his father had gone, and his mother was impatient for her release so that she could enter into a new, though essentially barren union with the man of her choice.

Youth. He smiled as he thought of it, a humorless quirking of the lips, unseen even by himself in the soft, trembling darkness which was the only night he had ever known. Schooling, always schooling and exercise and training. The psychological tests, the aptitude examinations and always the educational tapes at every leisure moment of every shift. The slow climb from manual worker status to administration; from administration to the coveted psych-police; from an officer to chief of P.P., from a nonentity to one of the select hierarchy; from a unit to a controller; from being helpless to being in a position to . . .

He stirred, fighting the thought, and switched on the lights, blinking for a moment as his eyes adapted to the glare. He rose, slipping from the pneumatic pallet with virile litheness, and stood for a moment, stretching and flexing his muscles, watching the reflected image of his naked figure in the clean surface of the metal wall. Then he shrugged and stepped towards his private shower.

The mist spray was hot, the lather quick to spring from his moistened body, and the following ten-second, ice-cold needle shower stung his flesh to full awareness. Still naked, he stepped from the warm-air blast and, as the droning current dried his body, stared hard at his reflection in the mirror. Vaguely he regretted that it was impossible to grow a beard and frowned as he examined his thick, short black hair. He turned as the attention call from the phone sounded above the soft whine of the dryer.

Still naked he walked into the other

room and picked up the handset.

'Yes?'

'Gregson?'

'Who else would it be? What do you want?'

'Quentin speaking.' There was a cold disapproval in the Captain's voice. 'I tried to get you at P.P. Headquarters.'

'I was off-shift and getting some sleep.' Gregson didn't alter his tone. 'I trust that this violation of privacy is important?'

'A psych-police officer is never private, you should know that.' Gregson bared his teeth as the Captain's voice echoed against his ear. 'Come up to the Bridge at once.'

'Can't it wait? I've a lot of routine stuff to get through and I'm supposed to be meeting Conway at Psycho.'

'Conway is here with me,' snapped the Captain. 'I'll expect you immediately.' The phone went dead with a decisive click and Gregson swore as he replaced the receiver.

The Captain was the oldest man aboard the Ship. Almost legendary, seen only by the hierarchy, a vague and, because of that, all the more impressive figure to the people, he lived in splendid isolation in his private apartment high towards No-Weight. Gregson knew him, and Conway, and Henderly the chief medical officer, but as far as Gregson knew, that was all.

The chief of psych-police stepped forward as the outer door opened, crossed the spacious room with long, easy strides, and took his place at the table without doing more than nod to the others present.

'Well, gentlemen, what's so important that you couldn't tell me over the phone?'

'I don't always trust the communication system of the Ship,' snapped the Captain. 'It isn't beyond the realms of possibility that some electronic engineer may have tapped the wires.'

'You think that?' Gregson leaned back and smiled towards the other two. Quentin leaned forward, his harsh, thin features stern and contemptuous beneath his mass of graying hair.

'You think that I'm a fool, Gregson?'

'No, but the suggestion is ridiculous,'

'Is it? Would you be surprised to learn that that very thing happened some forty years ago?' He stared at the dark-haired man sitting opposite. 'That, of course, would be before your time, but what has happened once could easily happen again.'

'I'm sorry,' said Gregson quietly. 'I keep forgetting that you are *old!*'

There was contempt in the way he said it but, beneath that contempt was a sick envy and the basic cause of his dislike for the Captain. Quentin was old, at least thirteenth generation, but, because he was the Captain and because it was essential to have at least one man who could take a long-term view of the Ship and its purposes the captains were always allowed to grow old.

'I'll ignore that remark,' said Quentin quietly, 'because I know what activated it. But at the same time I must ask you to remember who and what I am. I am the Captain, you are only the chief of psych-police.' The inference was obvious and Gregson bit his lips as he fought down his rage. Quentin picked up a thin, almost transparent sheet of paper from the table, glanced at it for a moment, then looked at the others.

'There was a Barb raid on the farming section of sector four,' he said flatly. 'As yet the news hasn't been allowed to disseminate and I trust that the occurrence will be kept as secret as possible.' He looked at Gregson. 'That is your job.'

'When did this raid take place?'

'Just before I called you — while you were asleep.' The taunt was unjustified and both Gregson and the Captain knew it. 'It was a small raid, three men and a woman, but it proves that the Barb menace isn't to be ignored as you gentlemen.' Quentin looked at Conway, 'have recommended.'

'I still recommend it,' said Conway. 'The Barbs are only a few discontented people who managed to evade elimination, and as they are all barren they will eventually die out from either starvation or natural death.'

'Is that correct, Henderly?'

'Broadly, yes.' The medical officer cleared his throat as he answered the

Captain. 'They are sterile, of course — everyone is over twenty-five — and they were old to begin with. Food, naturally, is their biggest problem. I have based my recommendation for the policy of ignoring them, on the twin factors of starvation and cannibalism.' He shrugged. 'They are hungry — so they must eat. We guard the messes — so they are forced to eat each other. That leads to mutual fear and, eventually, mutual destruction.'

'The psychological factors also lead me to agree with the existing policy,' said Conway importantly. 'Conditioned as they are to Ship procedure, their sense of guilt at betraying their own will lead to mental unrest and illogical behavior patterns. This, of course, will tend to disrupt their precarious social structure . . . if they have one, which I doubt.'

'They raided sector four,' reminded Quentin. 'That shows that they have learned to work together.'

'To a limited degree,' admitted Conway, 'but to me it is a sign that Henderly's summary of our policy is working.' He glanced towards Gregson. 'Do you agree?'

'They should be exterminated,' said Gregson flatly. He spoke again before the others could protest. 'I know all the arguments for and against and I know that we can't conduct a full-scale search and massacre in No-Weight without betraying the existence of the Barbs to the people.' He shrugged. 'I don't determine the policy of the Ship, I only carry it out, but I say that they should be exterminated.'

'Easier said than done,' commented Quentin dryly. 'Have you any suggestions as to how they could be eliminated without betraying their existence to the people?'

'Poisoned food? We could allow them to steal some yeast loaded with toxins or something. Henderly would know about that.'

'Impracticable,' snapped the medical officer. 'To begin with they would be suspicious of any food left for them to find. For another it would be waste.' He snorted. 'Your suggestion is ridiculous!'

'No suggestion is ridiculous,' said

Quentin sharply. He looked at Gregson. 'Have you any others?'

'No. As I told you, I have nothing to do with policy. I only carry out your orders.'

'I see.' Quentin looked again at the papers on his table. 'As you feel like that, Gregson, there is no apparent reason for me to keep you longer away from your duties. I'll notify you as to my decisions later.' He looked up in dismissal and Gregson felt his cheeks begin to burn in rage.

'Are you suggesting that I am not fit to sit in Council?'

'I suggest nothing — except that you are undoubtedly a busy man.' There was mockery in the way Quentin stared at the officer, mockery and a hint of something else, something cold and calculating. Gregson saw it, guessed what was happening, and restrained himself in time.

'I must remind you that I have but five officers to control a thousand times their number,' he said quietly. 'We have no weapons and must operate by stealth. I suggest that you gentlemen consider that in any plans you may choose to make.' He stepped away from the table. 'I will appreciate an early decision.'

'A moment.' Quentin fumbled among his papers, his thin hands a startling contrast to the youthful ones of the other men, and found a scrap of paper covered with close-set typescript. 'This belongs in your department.'

'What is it?' Gregson glanced down the paper, frowning as he followed the unfamiliar words, his lips moving with the unaccustomed exercise of reading. 'Is it important?'

'No.' Quentin took the sheet and scanned it with experienced eyes. 'An electronic engineer requests a personal interview with reference to Psycho.' The Captain shrugged. 'He refuses to state the nature of his business and remains so vague as to be almost incomprehensible.'

'Psycho?' Gregson stepped forward and took the paper, thrusting it into the top of his shorts. 'Something wrong?'

'Not that I know of,' said Conway sharply. He was jealous of his position as chief of Psycho. He looked at the

Captain. 'Why wasn't I informed of this?'

'You will be,' promised Gregson calmly. 'Just as soon as I've interviewed the man and decided whether he's psychotic or sincere.'

'That's for me to decide.'

'No. The psych-police are the ones to handle it, and besides,' Gregson allowed himself the luxury of sarcasm, 'you must be far too busy to bother with such trivial complaints.' He glanced from Conway's angry face to the calm one of the Captain. 'You want me to handle this?'

'Naturally,' snapped Quentin impatiently. 'I've quite enough to do now that the Barbs have taken to raiding without worrying about some low-grade worker who probably thinks that he can improve on the builders. Paper should never have been wasted on forwarding his request; there are proper channels in case of need.'

'May I see the request?' Conway half-rose, his hand extended, then sat back as the chief of psych-police stepped towards the door. 'Gregson! Didn't you hear me? I want to see that request.'

'You heard what the Captain said,

Conway.' Gregson paused by the door, his eyes insolent as he looked at the psychologist. 'Must I remind you again that I am a busy man?' He smiled. 'I'll leave you gentlemen to discuss the Barbs while I attend to my duties.'

He left them staring at the closing door.

6

Susan chuckled as she missed the medicine ball and watched it roll heavily into a corner. 'One up for you, Jay — but it isn't fair, you've more muscle than I have.'

'Have I?' Jay smiled down at her, his admiration for her trim perfection apparent in his eyes. 'Want to try something else then?'

'Yes.' She looked thoughtfully at him, trying not to admire his youthful grace. 'Let me see now, you're in ventilation and that means you spend a lot of time up in low gravity.' She smiled. 'I know! Let's play dueling!'

'No.'

'Why not? We can wear masks and jackets and use foils, or the practice knives if you prefer them.' She smiled at his hesitation. 'Come on, Jay. At least I don't want to try any bare-handed stuff with you — I wouldn't stand a chance.'

'I wouldn't say that,' he said, meeting her mood, then sobered again as he stared at her. 'Why do you want to play at dueling?'

'Why?' She shrugged. 'Why not? At least it may come in handy one day when I'm an old, unwanted woman. I may even have to fight a newcomer for my boyfriend.' She stepped closer to him. 'Will you be my boyfriend, Jay?'

'Stop it!' he said harshly. 'You don't know what you're saying.'

'Oh yes I do, Jay. I'm not a child any more and I know all about the facts of life. Next year I get married to someone approved by Genetics. I'll have children and we'll live in a family unit until I'm twenty-five, or maybe longer depending on how I like my husband. Then I'm free to do as I like.' She smiled at him, naked invitation in her soft brown eyes. 'Will you wait for me, Jay?'

'No.'

'Why not?' She touched his arm. 'You're not married, or at least you don't wear the banded shorts like Fred does, so what's to stop us making an agreement when I'm of age? Don't you like me, Jay?'

'You know damn well I like you.'

'You don't have to swear at me then.' She dropped her hand from his arm and stood, a sulky expression on her face, her foot tracing designs on the padded floor of the exercise room. 'Is there someone else?'

'No.'

'Are you sure, Jay?' She hesitated. 'If there is, well, I know that I shouldn't say anything, but . . . ' She bit her lip. 'Waste! Why are we talking like this?'

'No reason at all,' he said cheerfully. 'Here!' He threw her the ball. She caught it, an automatic reflex action, then flung it petulantly aside. 'I don't want to play anymore. Let's talk.'

'All right then,' he looked around at the crowded room. 'Here?'

'No. Let's find an unoccupied rec-room.' Before he could protest she had seized his arm and was leading him out into the corridor and up towards the next level where the common cubicles were. The fourth one she tried was empty and she switched on the light, closing the door and swinging over the 'engaged' indicator.

'There!' She sat down and smiled at him. 'Now we can really be alone.'

'You're crazy,' he said dispassionately. He stood by the door, staring down at her, noting her flushed features, glistening eyes and moist lips. 'You're playing with fire and don't know that you might be burned.'

'You won't burn me,' she said confidently. 'Jay, why be so cold? You know how I feel about you.'

'I know how you think you feel,' he corrected. He sat down, keeping well away from her, and a little muscle high on one cheek twitched as he fought to control his emotions. 'Look, Susan,' he said seriously. 'You don't want me to break the code, and you don't want to break it either. You're going to be married soon — why not wait until then?'

'But I'm not going to be able to marry you,' she said irritably. 'Why must you be so blind, Jay. You know what I want.'

'You want me to make love to you,' he stated. 'You're young and healthy and it's a perfectly natural reaction. But youthful immorality isn't a good thing. Susan, and you know it. Time enough for that when you've had your children and are out of marriageable status. You know what could happen if you were to have a child before your time?'

'Genetics would be annoyed,' she said defiantly. 'So what?'

'So the child would be aborted, I'd be punished for infringing the code, and you might lose the chance of having an approved child.' He shook his head. 'No, Susan, we daren't do it.'

He was right, of course, and both of them knew it. A strong race cannot be an immoral race, not when excess would tend to weaken the very hope of the new generation. Shame was unknown on the Ship, but indoctrination had set up a rigid code which no one in his right mind would think of transgressing. The trouble was that young people in love are seldom in their right mind.

'You talk just like father,' Susan said bitterly. 'All about what I should and should not do, but never a word about what I'd like to do.' She turned to him, very young and very lovely. 'Oh, Jay! How can you ask me to wait so long?'

'We must.' He stood up out of reach of her outstretched hands. 'What did your father say about me?'

'The usual.' She was annoyed with him for changing the subject and, woman-like, annoyed too that he hadn't found her attractions irresistible to logic and good sense. 'He says that you're too old for me and that I should settle down to being a good wife and mother to some young dolt I haven't even seen yet.'

'You'll see him soon,' promised Jay. 'You youngsters are thrown together when you near marriageable status. You might even go to another sector, or the boys be brought here.' He smiled at her expression. 'Don't worry, you know that you'll be able to take a choice; you won't be limited to one.'

'But supposing they send me out of the sector!' She rose and stepped towards him, her arms circling his neck, her lips hungry for his. 'Jay! What if I don't see you again!'

He didn't like to think about it. He

didn't like to think about anything, not when she was so near to him and every atom of his body was crying out for her. His life was a lonely one; a marriageless though not a celibate state was a requirement of the psych-police, and he found little interest in the casual relationships which Merrill favored so much.

And he was in love with Susan.

The speakers saved him. They crackled into life and a voice, cold and emotionless, repeated his code number over and over again, sounding in every room for every sector, demanding and urgent.

'X112 . . . X112 . . . X112 . . . '

'That's my number.' Jay hesitated a moment; then, his indoctrination overcoming his natural desires, gently unfolded her arms from about his neck. 'I must go, Susan. They want me to report in immediately.'

'Must you?' She clung to him again. 'Don't go yet, Jay.'

'I must.' He moved away from her. 'That's my emergency call. Something's wrong and they want me.'

'Waste!' She stepped back, her eyes

hungry as they searched his face. 'Can't they do without you just for this once?'

'They wouldn't be calling me if they could.' He held out his hand. 'Goodbye, Susan.'

'Goodbye?' She frowned and, stepping close to him, gripped his arm so hard that her fingers dug into his flesh. 'Do you love me, Jay?'

'I must report in.' He moved towards the door, then hesitated as she dragged at his arm.

'I asked you a question, Jay. Do you love me?'

He didn't answer. He stared at her, afraid to say the words which came so naturally to his lips for fear of what they could bring, and yet more afraid to lie. He swallowed, shook off her arm and stepped out into the corridor, leaving the door of the rec-room swinging wide.

The call was, as he expected, from headquarters and the public voice fell into silence as he contacted the desk.

'West reporting. What's the trouble?'

'No trouble,' said Carter, the officer on stand-by duty. 'Gregson wants you.

Routine job I think, but you'd better get back fast — he's flaming.'

'Let him flame,' snapped Jay disrespectfully. 'I'll be there as soon as I can and not a second before.' He heard Carter chuckle as he hung up the receiver. The trip up to low gravity didn't take long and his red, ventilation engineer's shorts passed by through the guarded doors towards No-Weight. This was a part of the Ship which was little used. The circumference was too small for spacious rooms, and the gravity too low for real comfort. Here were the stores, the huge water containers, the massive ventilation pipes and power conduits. They lay all around the odd, no-man's-land of No-Weight, the central axis which in effect was a hollow tube filled with a tangled mass of girders and stanchions, struts and braces, the pivot of the Ship around which the rest swung.

Jay passed quickly down a long corridor running parallel to No-Weight, kicking with practiced ease at the metal walls as he glided along, careful not to impart too high a velocity to his body.

Men had died through failing to take that precaution. They had forgotten that, while they were apparently weightless, they still had mass. Mass has inertia and inertia had caused splintered bones and crushed skulls as bodies, moving too fast, had collided against the unyielding structure of the Ship.

Before leaving the communicating tube, Jay reversed his shorts and, dressed again in his official uniform, passed the guard and moved down into sector three. Rapidly he made his way down the levels, past the gardens, the farms, the residential cubicles, along the com-tube and into P.P. headquarters.

Gregson was waiting for him when he arrived.

The chief looked up from his desk as Jay entered, gestured to a seat, and continued to leaf through a batch of reports. He read slowly, biting his lips with impatience as he scanned the thin, erasable plastic sheets. 'Why can't they put this stuff on audible tape?' he asked no one in particular.

Jay shrugged, not answering and

guessing that Gregson didn't really want a reply. 'You sent for me?'

'Yes. What kept you so long?'

'I was in sector five on unofficial duty.'

'I know. Merrill called in and reported seeing you.' Gregson stared at the young man. 'He seemed worried, said something about a young girl you took to a rec-room.'

'Did he?' Jay shifted a little beneath Gregson's stare, half-annoyed at himself for feeling a sense of guilt.

'Merrill wants to mind his own business.'

'It is his business. As official officer of the sector, it's his duty to safeguard the young. How serious is it?'

'Not serious at all. Forget it.'

'You certain about that? Sometimes these things get out of hand and you know the penalties for breaking the code when it comes to a thing like that.'

'You don't have to tell me the code,' snapped Jay irritably. 'I've said that you can forget it. It's all over. I doubt if I'll ever see her again.'

'I hope that you mean that,' said

Gregson seriously. 'I can protect my officers to some extent, but no one can protect you from Genetics if they bring an immorality charge. It means being referred to Psycho. With anyone else it could mean just a downgrading, but with you ... ' Gregson made an expressive gesture with the edge of his hand and Jay knew exactly what he meant. Psych-Police officers couldn't be down-graded; they knew too much, and that left elimination as the only possible punishment. He swallowed.

'It's finished. I mean it.'

'I know how you feel,' Gregson said with unusual sympathy. 'You're young, she's young, and that's as far as you think.' He hesitated. 'Do you want a transfer to another sector? I could switch you with Norton if you like.'

'No thanks, it won't be necessary. I know the people in sector five and can work more efficiently there.' He looked at his chief. 'Is that what you called me in to tell me?'

'No.'

'Then?'

'Merrill phoned in after your call went out and I thought I'd mention it while you were here.' Gregson picked up something from his desk. 'I've got a job for you. The others have had their assignment cards but this is the only one in your unofficial sector.' He threw a strip of plastic towards Jay. 'Here, you know what to do.'

Jay nodded and picked up the plastic strip. He had seen them before, lots of them, and he had long ago lost any emotion he might have once had. The strip was from Psycho and contained the full data on someone's life. It had been rejected, thrown out . . . and as he looked down at it, Jay could see the broad red star smeared all over the smooth surface. The red star, which meant that a person had been weighed, considered — and found wanting.

Casually he read the name and number of the person he was to kill: *Curtway, George. 14/4762. Electronics.*

Susan's father.

★ ★ ★

There were times when Jay hated his job. Not many, for like all Ship personnel he was efficient and took a pride in his job, but sometimes, like now, he wished that he had belonged to anything but the psych-police. It was his fault, of course; he should never have allowed himself to become so intimate with people who, by the very nature of things, must inevitably become his victims. But self-blame, like self-justification, were both a waste of time. He still had to kill Susan's father.

Had to. Indoctrination, conditioning, his own pride in his work and his knowledge that, should he refuse, he would be 'eliminated' as unfit, left him no choice. George Curtway had to die.

He changed before entering sector five, reversing his black shorts for the red ones of the ventilation engineer he was supposed to be in his unofficial sector, and made his way down towards the lower levels. Usually on such a mission he felt a certain excitement, the thrill of the hunter stalking the hunted, his wits against those of the selected victim with the rules heavily in his favor. And yet, even with the protection his official status gave him, there was always an element of danger.

He could be clumsy. He could bungle, be seen by witnesses, or do such a poor job of staging the 'accident' that he would be judged inefficient and be eliminated in turn. Murder, even with the victim unaware and unprepared, was not always easy.

But this time, instead of the thrill, the warmth of released adrenaline, he felt a vague regret and a disinclination to do what must be done. He recognized the danger and deliberately focused his mind on his victim, forcing himself to forget Susan, their close friendship, their love and everything about them. Her father had to die and, as far as Jay was concerned, that was all there was to it. He felt a little better by the time he reached the lower levels where the games and recreation rooms were.

George wasn't in any of the rec-rooms, nor the exercise rooms, nor in the private cubicle his status allowed. Jay knew that he could locate the man by inquiring at the work-office. Curtway could have been out on a job somewhere — but to do that would be to leave a clue and maybe arouse suspicion. He was staring into the mess, trying to find the man he was looking for, when someone touched his arm.

'Jay! I didn't expect to see you again so soon. Don't you ever work?' it was Susan, the last person he wished to see. Looking down at her he wished that they had never met.

'Hello. Susan.' Deliberately he made his voice casual.

'Eaten yet?'

'Not yet.' She linked her arm through his and smiled up into his face. 'Let's eat together, shall we?'

'If you like.' Casually he slipped his arm from hers and they moved towards a vacant table. He ordered without paying much attention to the menu. Susan kept glancing at him, seeming about to speak once or twice, then, pushing aside her empty plates touched his arm.

'Anything wrong, Jay?'

'Wrong?' He forced himself to smile at

her, annoyed with himself for betraying his emotions. 'No, of course not. What makes you think that?'

'Your appetite for one thing.' She gestured towards his unfinished meal. 'I've never known you to be so slow before.'

'I'm not hungry.'

'Then you shouldn't have sat down to eat.' Susan glanced over the mess hall. 'Better finish it up, Jay, or someone will accuse you of waste. There's a man standing over by the far wall who seems very interested in you as it is.'

'Is there?' He didn't turn his head to look, guessing that it was Susan the man was interested in, not her escort. But he finished his meal all the same, refusing a sweet and sipping his water while Susan spooned up the last of her synthetic fruit.

'When am I going to see you again, Jay?' Susan smiled as she leaned forward and touched his hand. 'After shift?'

'I doubt it.'

'When then? Tomorrow?'

'I don't think so.' He looked down at the table as he spoke. 'I'm pretty busy right now and it's hard to know just when I'll be free.' He stared at her, his face expressionless. 'In fact, Susan, you'd better not rely on seeing me again.'

'What!' She stared at him a moment, her hand gripping his arm; then she laughed. 'Jay! Don't say things like that!'

'I mean it, Susan.' Deliberately he removed her hand from his arm.

'You're joking! You couldn't mean it — not after what we've been to each other.' Her eyes searched his face. 'Please, Jay, say that you're not serious.'

'I am serious,' he said flatly. 'There's no future in it for either of us and it would be best if we never met again.'

'Jay!' There was hurt in her voice, the deep pain of outraged emotion and broken illusion. He heard it, knew that he was being deliberately cruel, and yet, at the same time, that it was the only thing he could do. He stared into her soft, brown eyes.

'Listen, Susan,' he said curtly. 'Let's not get foolish over this. We've had fun and I've enjoyed knowing you, but it's all over now. Let's forget it, shall we?'

'Jay!' For a moment he thought that she was going to break down. Tears filled her eyes and her hands showed white at the knuckles as she gripped the edge of the table. Then pride came to her rescue, the outraged pride of any woman who has had her affection flung back into her face, and together with that pride came anger. She stiffened with youthful dignity.

'All right, Jay. If that's all it meant to you.' She paused, hopefully, and for a moment he was tempted to say the word which would remove her pain and restore her smile. He didn't say it.

'It was fun,' he repeated stubbornly. 'It should never have become so serious. It's best that we part now before any damage is done.'

'I see.' She stared down at the table, then, with a brave attempt at casualness, glanced around the mess hall. 'Don't bother to justify yourself, Jay. As you said, it was fun. I've been a fool, I suppose, but . . . ' She swallowed. 'This is the end, then?'

'Yes.'

He didn't look at her as she rose from

the table. He didn't follow her with his eyes as she stumbled towards the door and to the privacy of the nearest unoccupied rec-room. She would cry, he thought dully. She would vent her emotion in tears, hate him, despise him and then, after a while, forget him.

But the thought didn't make him happy.

He sat for a while, sipping his water, trying to bring his mind back into focus and the job at hand. There was no particular hurry, he knew that, but he wanted to get the thing over and done with long before the three-day period of grace was over. The hard part was over; he had managed to make Susan hate him, and all that was left was a simple job of murder.

He was leaving the hall when a man stepped forward and collided with him with sufficient force to send him reeling against a table.

'You!' The man pressed his hand to his side, his face distorted with synthetic pain. 'Why don't you watch where you're going?'

'Sorry.' Jay was in no mood for argument and he was in a hurry. He tried to step past the man, then halted as a hand gripped his arm.

'Not so fast! You hurt me.'

'So what?' Jay stared at the sullen-faced man in the brown shorts. 'I apologized.'

'That's not good enough,' said Sam Aldway deliberately. 'It's about time your sort were taught that you can't go around hurting people.' He looked at the little crowd which had gathered around them. 'You all saw what he did,' he shouted. 'I say that it isn't good enough.'

'Take your hands off me!' Jay jerked his arm, then, as the man tried to grab him again, pushed him back. 'I told you to keep your paws to yourself.'

'You hit me!' Sam appealed again to the crowd. 'You all saw him hit me.'

'Don't be a fool.' Jay fought his rising anger and spoke as calmly as he could. 'We bumped into each other, and if I hurt you, then I'm sorry. I've apologized — I can't do more. Now shut up and leave me alone.' He stepped forward, trying to thrust his way through the press of bodies, then turned as a hand clawed at his shoulder. 'I told you to leave me alone.'

'Oh no you don't.' Sam grinned, conscious of being the center of attraction, and spoke directly to Jay. 'You're a dirty, stinking, lousy waster,' he said loudly. 'And I want to know what you're going to do about it.'

It was so raw as to be ludicrous. The man was an arrogant, loud-mouthed fool, and he was clumsily trying to force Jay into a duel. Jay knew it, knew too that he, with his superior training, would be certain to win, and for a moment was tempted to work off some of his frustration and anger in violent physical combat. He shook his head and laughed.

'So I'm a waster, am I? Then why don't you call the psych-police?'

'You mean that you refuse to fight?' Incredulous anger twisted Sam's face into an animal-mask of hate. 'Why, you rotten coward — you call yourself a man? I've called you a waster. Did you hear that? *A dirty waster!* I'll show you what I do with wasters.'

Before Jay could guess what he was about to do, Sam had stepped forward and swung his open hand against Jay's cheek. The sound of the slap was followed by a startled hush, a hush broken by the soggy impact of bone against flesh.

Normally, Jay would never have done it. Normally his innate caution and the grim necessity to put his assignment above all else would have forced him to swallow the insult, accept the inevitable sneers of cowardice, and to go on his way.

But he was still raw from his parting with Susan, sick with the knowledge of what he had yet to do, and his emotions overrode good sense as he swung his fist deep into the flesh of the other's stomach. Coldly he stared at the writhing man at his feet, knowing that now he had gone too far to back out. There was no brawling in the Ship, there couldn't be, not with five thousand people living too close together. A brawl could start a riot which would ruin irreplaceable material, injure essential workers and kill the innocent parents of the new generations.

Like it or not, Jay had to fight a duel.

7

The stadium was on the lowest level next to the exercise rooms. From a sanded floor rows of tiered seats sloped up to a high roof and, when Jay and Sam arrived followed by the interested crowd, a couple of women were fighting a bloody battle with razor-edged knives to the amusement of the usual watchers.

Both well over thirty, they fought with the ferocity of tigers, the gleaming blades slashing at yielding flesh as they spun and dodged on the absorbent sand. From the crowd came a soft half-sigh, half-groan as one of them slipped, falling on to one knee, her knife had resting for a moment on the floor. Quickly the other moved in, her blade a lancing arc as the needle point thrust through skin and fat, muscle and sinew towards the pulsing heart beneath. Triumphantly, she grinned towards the audience, kissed her bloodstained fingers at the referee and walked staggeringly towards the exit.

Jay watched her, trying to guess from her wounds whether she would be healed or eliminated. From her age, the blood she had lost, and the obvious skill with which she had used her weapon, he guessed the latter. Expert duelists, while encouraged up to a point, became dangerous when they lost their sense of proportion and vied with each other in the number of their kills. The Ship had no room for blood-crazed beasts.

The ref checked them in, making the routine inspection of their forearms, and asking the usual questions.

'Are you both certain that you can't settle your differences in any other way?'

'I'm willing to call it off,' said Jay. He looked at Sam. 'And you?'

'Not a chance.'

'I see that this is your first duel.' The ref stared at Jay's unmarked forearm, then at the five dots on Sam's. 'As a first-timer you have the choice of weapons. Also,' he stared hard at Sam, 'you will not be killed in this encounter.' He looked back at Jay. 'How will you fight?'

'Bare handed.' Jay had no intention of getting cut or slashed by knife or machete and, aside from anything else, he was skilled in the art of unarmed combat. Already he regretted having agreed to fight at all; it was too easy to be injured in the stadium, and even the most experienced fighter could fall victim to an unlucky blow. Without weapons, however, there was little chance of anything worse than a beating up.

Their turn was scheduled for after the next bout and he waited impatiently while a young, optimistic man just out of marriageable status took on a well-muscled woman about ten years his senior. Fights between mixed couples, while rare, were not uncommon. Equality between the sexes demanded utter lack of distinction, though, as in this case, the bout was usually fought with padded clubs which were painful enough but capable of inflicting little more than a bruise. In effect it was a comedy turn and the crowd greeted the young man's defeat with catcalls turning to ribald cheers as the woman, dropping her club, picked up her opponent and carried him tenderly from the arena.

Jay smiled, guessing that another domestic problem had been solved the hard way, then lost his smile as the referee gestured towards them.

'Right. You two are on now. Remove your sandals, walk out five paces apart and, when you reach the center, turn and fight.'

Jay hesitated, glancing at Sam, then, as the other made no move, he shrugged and strode out into the arena. The space was about twenty yards long and fifteen wide, brilliantly lit so that the surrounding faces of the watching crowd merged into a formless blur. The attendants had cleared away the debris of the previous bouts, raking the sand and removing the discarded weapons, and the fine grit felt warm and smooth between his naked toes. Now that the moment had arrived he felt calm and, as he strode forward, he evaluated his chances. There was a slight disadvantage in coming out first for he could not be certain just where Sam would be, but that disadvantage would be offset by his superior skill. He turned as he reached the halfway mark, springing to one side and poising on the balls of his feet. Sam glared at him, paused just as he was about to spring; then, before he could recover his balance, Jay had stepped forward and slammed his fist towards the other's jaw.

He missed, but he had expected it, and as Sam swayed to one side, his other hand drove forward towards his stomach. He grinned as he felt the blow smash home and followed it with two more, one to the head and one to the heart. Crowding forward so as to keep Sam off-balance, he smashed at him with all the force of his back and shoulder muscles.

For a moment he thought that the fight was over almost before it had begun. Sam gulped, tried to cover, then, as blood gushed from his pulped nose, screamed with rage and flung himself forward, his hands reaching for Jay's face and throat.

Immediately Jay was fighting for his life.

It was dirty fighting, but it was more than that. It was the double attack possible only to a trained fighter and, as Jay felt the other's hands smash at vital nerves, he felt the first doubt as to his success. The double attack he could handle, he used it himself, but as they fought, he became aware that Sam knew far more than any ordinary duelist should.

A knee thrust at his groin at the same time that stiffened fingers stabbed at his eyes. He twisted to avoid the knee, knocked aside the threatening fingers, and tasted blood as a lowered skull smashed into his face. Again the knee jerked towards him, and in avoiding it he fell victim to a slash from the edge of a palm directed towards his throat. It was the double attack, the system of two separate blows at the same time directed towards different parts of the anatomy: knee to groin, fingers to eyes, blow to stomach, skull against face, edge of palm towards throat, without pause or time for the victim to recover his balance.

For a while they wove like fencers, body against body, arms and legs moving in smooth, synchronized rhythm as they delivered and countered blows, their sweat-streaked bodies glistening beneath the glare of the lights. Then, as he felt his left arm go numb, Jay broke away and ran towards the end of the arena.

Sam was dangerous. Avoiding the other's rush, Jay frantically massaged life and feeling back into his numbed arm. How or where the duelist had learned of the subtle nerve-blows which could maim and paralyze, Jay didn't know, but his numbed arm gave shocking proof that he had learned them. Jay knew them, all the psych-police did, but that information was carefully kept from the Ship personnel. It was too easy to kill a man with that knowledge and, as he stared at the crouching figure of his opponent, Jay revised his previous opinions as to the certainty of his victory.

There is a state of mind indispensable to a fighter if he hopes to win. Contempt has no place and neither has indifference; everything has to be sublimated to a single objective, every emotion and thought fined to a needle point directed to one aim. To kill. To rend and tear, to smash and destroy, to crush and vanquish. Sam had it; it was apparent in his eyes, his mouth, the very set and stance of his body. Before he could hope to meet the man on equal terms, Jay had to acquire it too.

For him it was simple.

He moved forward as life returned to his numbed arm, dodged a handful of sand flung towards his eyes, and struck out with his left fist. Sam knocked aside the blow, gripped the wrist, twisted, turned and suddenly brought the trapped limb down hard against his shoulder. Normally that would have broken the arm, would have snapped it at the elbow and left Jay crippled and helpless, but Sam was up against no normal fighter.

Jay leaped up and forward as Sam turned and, just as he felt the pressure being applied to his elbow, the fingers of his right hand curled beneath Sam's chin, probed for a moment at the knotted muscles of the throat, then dug in with savage viciousness.

The rest was merely for the benefit of the crowd.

It was butchery, cold, calculated, and serving both to cover up the effects of the nerve-blow and to vent Jay's own hate and rage. He slammed his fists against Sam's face and head, opened a cut over one eye, split his lips and, with one final blow to the jaw, finished the unequal combat.

He walked towards the referee, leaving the duelist unconscious on the reddening sand.

'A good bout,' complimented the referee. 'I thought that you'd be in trouble there — Aldway's nasty fighter, but you handled yourself well.' He picked up a red-tipped stylus. 'Hold out your arm.'

Silently Jay held out his left forearm for the referee to brand him with the red dot. It was a nuisance, but he could have it removed at Medical, and to protest would be to arouse suspicion. He was donning his sandals when someone called to him.

'Jay! I didn't think that you went in for dueling.'

It was George Curtway, and the sight of him brought back all the unaccustomed indecision which Jay had managed to rid himself of in the arena. Slowly he fastened the catch of his sandal.

'So it was Sam Aldway you were fighting.' George stared down at the pale face of the duelist as he was carried out by the attendants. 'You want to watch him, Jay. He'll never forgive you for besting him. What happened?'

'He wanted to pick a quarrel,' said Jay shortly. 'He picked on me and I was lucky enough to win.' He crossed to the water spray and washed the blood from his face. 'Busy, George?'

'Just finished. We had a sticky job up in low-weight — condensation in the junction boxes — but I'm free now.' He hesitated, staring at Jay. 'Look. Jay, there's something I've been meaning to talk to you about. Are you free now?'

'Yes.' Jay dried his face and hands in the warm-air blast. 'What is it?'

'I'll tell you later.' George stared at the people around them. 'Have you eaten?'

'Yes.'

'That's a pity. I'm starving and we could have eaten together.' George frowned, 'Tell you what. Meet me in my cubicle. There's a viewer there so you won't be bored, and I'll join you as soon as I've had a meal. Right?'

Jay nodded and, leaning against the wall, watched the electronics man thrust his way through the inevitable crowd around the stadium and turn down a corridor. It was luck, he thought dully.

The man he was looking for had found him first, had even arranged a rendezvous for his own death, though he couldn't know that, of course, Jay should have been pleased, but somehow he felt even more despondent than before. He started as a man touched his arm.

'I watched you in the arena,' said the man thickly. 'A good bout. Want to try another?'

He was still young, scarred a little and the inside of his left arm was dotted with the red marks of the experienced duelist. Looking at him Jay recognized the type, a natural born fighter, a man whose only pleasure was in pitting his strength and skill against others. Jay shook his head.

'Sorry, but no.'

'A pity.' The man shrugged, not

annoyed at the refusal but vaguely regretful at a lost opportunity. 'No need to make it a death-bout. Just a friendly battle to work off energy.' He looked hopefully at Jay. 'Some other time, perhaps?'

'Perhaps.' Jay watched him move towards a small crowd waiting for seats in the stadium, half-amused at the man's sincerity, and mentally comparing him to Aldway. Sam was dangerous, a man who would have to be eliminated before he made too big a nuisance of himself. The other was an integral part of the economy of the Ship.

Jay sighed and made his way towards Curtway's private cubicle.

8

Quentin, Captain of the Ship, sat at the head of his desk and stared at the men sitting before him with amusement tinged with contempt. They were so obvious, so transparent, so young. Conway, swollen with his own importance at being in charge of Psycho. Henderly, jealous of the psychologist and yet conscious of his own superiority. Malick, Chief of Genetics, the little god of a little world. Gregson, hard and implacable, cold and ruthless, toying with intrigue and insanely envious, not of the Captain, but of what he represented. Folden, Chief of Supply.

The hierarchy of the Ship.

Quentin let them sit in silence for a while, calm in the knowledge of his own superiority, and yet, even as he sat, his eyes were never still. Old those eyes might be, but they had lost none of their sharpness and they saw far more than any of the men before him imagined. Quentin was no fool.

He rustled the thin papers on his desk, selected one, scanned it more for appearances than for any real need to remind himself of what it contained; then dropping it, stared at Gregson.

'Any further news on the elimination of the Barbs?'

'None.' Gregson scarcely troubled to disguise his impatience. 'As yet three schemes have been submitted to me for approval. All are verging on the ludicrous in their total disregard of facts. I can only assume that the originators of the schemes must be trying a feeble joke at my expense.'

'I submitted one of those schemes,' said Henderly harshly. 'What was the matter with it?'

'The same as with all of them.' Gregson shrugged at the medical officer's expression of anger. 'Of the three, two advocated the offer of amnesty to the Barbs if they would return to their sectors. I need hardly emphasize the stupidity of that suggestion. They know full well what will happen to them if they agree to return. The third contained some wild scheme to electrify the stanchions and girders of No-Weight.'

'That was my suggestion,' said Conway. 'What's wrong with it?'

'Better ask the electronic engineers that. I did. They tell me that even if it were possible to divert sufficient current to No-Weight to send a lethal voltage through the fabric, it would be impossible to insulate it from the rest of the Ship without extensive alterations.'

'I see.' Quentin spoke before Conway could express his anger at the sneering tone of contempt Gregson had used. 'I assume, of course, that you have a better suggestion?'

'I have.'

'May we hear it? Or does the Chief of Psych-Police consider that his Captain is too stupid to understand it?'

'Stupidity is a relative term,' said Gregson stiffly. 'Perhaps one of my officers would consider you stupid if ever you met him in the arena.'

'If I was ever so unwise as to place myself in that position,' said Quentin quietly, 'then I would be something more than stupid. Your suggestion?'

'Seal No-Weight and search it from end to end with armed men given orders to kill everyone they find.' Gregson shrugged at their instinctive recoiling from the use of weapons. 'If you don't like to arm the men, then I have another plan. Seal the area just the same and flood it with lethal gas. Exterminate the Barbs for the vermin they are.'

'And how would you get rid of the gas afterwards?' Quentin gestured for Folden to remain silent. 'Have you considered that?'

'Chemistry isn't my department. Is it possible to use a neutralizing agent for the gas? Or perhaps we could extract the poisoned air and replace it with fresh?'

'No to both suggestions,' said Folden impatiently. 'We know of no such neutralizing agent, and to evacuate the air would be criminal waste.'

'Justifiable waste.'

'Criminal,' insisted Folden. 'We could replace the air, yes, but to evacuate anything from the Ship would be to disturb the ecology. I must veto any such suggestion.'

'Why not arm the searchers, then? Or would that be criminal waste too?' Gregson glared at the Chief of Supply, sarcasm heavy in his voice.

'What would you arm them with, Gregson?' Quentin's voice, though calm, had a peculiar carrying quality. 'Knives? Clubs?'

'Guns, of course, what else?'

'I take it that you mean high-velocity pistols. Have you ever fired one?'

'You know that I haven't. No one has. Weapons are forbidden aboard the Ship.'

'Exactly, and for a very good reason.' Quentin sighed as if finding the explanation tedious. 'First, even if you had one, I doubt if you could hit anything with it. Before a pistol can be used, training and practice are essential. Second, even if you could use them, I would never allow them to be fired within the Ship. The damage they would cause to the structure would be worse than tolerating the Barbs. You seem to have no idea of the impact force of a bullet and certainly none of the vulnerability of the Ship itself. No, Gregson, I cannot accept either of your suggestions.'

'Then what are you going to do, let the Barbs alone to raid the farms and laugh at us?'

'The Barbs are a minor nuisance and any plan which necessitates too great an expenditure of time or material would be defeating its own end. However, Henderly has a plan which I am considering and which may lead to their successful elimination. Incidentally, Gregson, I shouldn't have to remind you that the very existence of the Barbs is proof of your own inefficiency.'

'Twenty people have fled to No-Weight during the past ten years,' snapped Gregson. 'That is less than two per cent of the total disposable population during that time. I would hardly consider that inefficient.'

'You are at liberty to think as you wish.' Quentin selected another paper from the litter before him. 'Malick! Your report on population disturbs me. Explain.'

'We are reaching saturation point,' said

the saturnine-faced head of Genetics. 'As far as possible we have managed to avoid inbreeding by shift of personnel and rigorous mating control. However, as time passes, it is getting more and more difficult to select suitable partners for the new generation. Some inbreeding has become inevitable, and more will be necessary during future years.'

'Is that bad?' Henderly leaned forward, his eyes bright with professional interest. 'Surely the inferior strains have been eliminated by now?'

'Naturally, but there is always some danger in inbreeding; the possibility of atavism is higher than normal and certain nervous disorders can be expected if we continue as at present.'

'I don't understand this.' Folden stared at the chief of genetics. 'As far as I can see, inbreeding is unavoidable. Didn't the builders take all that into account?'

'They did.'

'Then what's the trouble?'

'The trouble is simply one of time and circumstances.' Like Quentin, Malick seemed tired of having to explain. 'The

125

builders determined, quite rightly, that in order to keep the race healthy we must concentrate on youth, not age. As far as Genetics is concerned, a man or woman has served the purpose of their existence as soon as they have mated and given birth to children. We are only interested in the new generation; the old merely serves to maintain the Ship, and is expendable as soon as others grow to take its place.' He glanced towards Gregson. 'You know all about that and you also know that Psycho determines the population figures and personnel for elimination on the basis of general unfitness or sheer need of living space. So many new births allowed per year, therefore so many deaths necessary to make room for the new life.'

'One hundred and thirty new births per year,' said Gregson, partly because he didn't like being ignored and partly to show his own knowledge. 'Of the necessary deaths, about a half are eliminated by dueling. The remainder are taken care of by my officers.' He shrugged. 'It works out at about a death a month per sector.'

'What has that got to do with inbreeding?' snapped Conway impatiently. 'What are you getting at, Malick?'

'Simply this. As all female personnel are automatically sterilized when leaving marriageable status, we are confined to a very limited age-group for breeding purposes. We have young parents, they mate at optimum age, but we are unable to use the same parents more than once. In other words, a boy marries a girl, gives her children, and then is prevented from entering into a fruitful marriage with a second woman.' Malick shrugged. 'We have bred for optimum characteristics, of course, and have managed to breed out all hereditary diseases, mental instability, and certain undesirable physical deformities. We have bred a race of highly intelligent, physically perfect men and women, but in so doing we have also given ourselves a first-class problem.'

'I begin to see what you're driving at,' Henderly said. 'Nervous potential?'

'Exactly. They appear to have had the same trouble back on Earth when they were toying with the breeding of race horses. They bred for speed at any price, and wound up with walking bundles of nervous tension almost impossible to control. There is nothing basically wrong in selective breeding if the original stock is sound. The trouble starts when you breed for certain characteristics. We have bred for an adventurous type with a high survival factor and amazingly fast reflexes. We've got that, but we've also got what goes with it.'

'Don't you trust Psycho?' interrupted Quentin softly.

'What?' Malick blinked and stared at the Captain. 'Of course I trust Psycho, but that doesn't prevent me from asking myself what is going to happen. What is the good of breeding an adventurous type when there is nowhere for them to go adventuring? How can we control highly strung, sensitive men and women when they are surrounded by a limited existence almost calculated to drive them into a frenzy of frustration?' He almost seemed about to burst into tears as he asked the questions. 'I'm not questioning the builders

128

— obviously they knew what they were doing — but to me it seems all wrong. The Ship isn't the place for the type of human we've bred. We should have gone in for morons, dull-witted clods who would be content to eat, sleep and mate like the animals they would be. You can't give a man a keen brain and a perfect body and then prevent him from using them. Not if you want to avoid trouble you can't.'

'Calm yourself, Malick.' Quentin smiled with quiet satisfaction as the Chief of Genetics relaxed. 'That's better. It is foolish and a waste of energy to torment yourself with questions of what may never happen.'

He picked up and scanned another of the papers before him. 'Conway, are you satisfied that everything is normal with Psycho?'

'Of course it is, why shouldn't it be?' The automatic defense of the psychologist almost made the old man smile. 'Nothing is wrong in my department.'

'Are you certain of that?' Quentin stared at Conway with peculiar intentness. 'Something in your report makes me wonder.

There is a slight alteration in the ratio between permissible births and recommended eliminations. Have you noticed it yourself?'

'Oh, that?' Conway dismissed it with a shrug. 'Simply explained. The incidence of dueling has risen during the past few years, probably due to the very thing Malick has been telling us about. Naturally, as there is more room for new life the number of permissible births has risen also.'

'Does that also account for the reduction in the number of recommended eliminations?'

'What else?' Conway seemed genuinely amazed at the question. 'We remove the cards of those killed in duels, you know, and Psycho automatically allows for them.'

'That would hardly account for the fall,' reminded Quentin. 'The fact that several deaths have occurred from dueling would not alter the fact that others would be considered unfit by Psycho. Old men, for example, those who have reached their fortieth year.

'Perhaps, said Conway doubtfully. 'I hadn't thought of it like that.

'I can't see that it makes any difference,' said Gregson. 'We have to eliminate about a hundred and thirty men and women a year. The fact that more of them are being killed in the stadium doesn't alter the fact. It only makes the job of the psych-police a little easier.'

'Of course.' Quentin rustled his papers again, apparently accepting the explanation. 'Your report interests me, Folden. I will discuss it with you later, after I have had time to check certain details.'

'My report of the supply position?' Folden looked at the Captain. 'I've already checked everything possible and the inference is plain. Normal wastage has reduced our potential to a disturbingly low figure. I — '

'I said that I will discuss it with you later.' Quentin silenced the Chief of Supply with a gesture, conscious of the open interest of the others. 'Have any of you anything further to say at this meeting?'

'The tapes,' blurted Malick, then

stopped as the others stared at him.

'Yes?' encouraged Quentin. 'You were saying?'

'I don't know if my memory is bad, or whether the tapes now shown on the children's screens are different from what they were, but I can't make sense of them.'

Malick stared a little helplessly at the incredulous faces of the men around him. 'I know that the educational tapes are routed automatically to various sectors and subsectors by Psycho, but to me it seems that they are totally at variance to what is normal.'

'How do you mean?' said Quentin sharply. 'Explain yourself.'

'Well, you know that we've always had tapes showing scenes of old Earth, the idea being, I suppose, that the children would remember the planet of their origin. But now those tapes seem to be in far greater detail than ever before. There are entire sequences of growth and decay, the balance of insect life to animal, the interplay of flora and fauna. There have even been scenes of the actual trapping and butchering of animals for meat!' Malick shuddered. 'They were disgusting! Who in their right mind would ever consider eating meat, anyway?'

'You might,' said the Captain gently, 'if you were starving and meat was the only edible food.'

'The only meat aboard the Ship,' said Malick tightly, 'is the personnel. Are you advocating cannibalism?'

'I advocate nothing; I merely answered your question, and you are quite wrong in your statement. There is meat aboard the Ship other than the men and women you have bred.'

'I don't count the animals in deep-freeze,' snapped Malick irritably. 'They are in the sealed areas, apart from the Ship proper.'

'They are still meat, just the same.'

'That has nothing to do with it. Those tapes are contaminating the minds of the young and they should be stopped.' Malick stared accusingly at Conway. 'You are in charge of Psycho. Why don't you get the electronic engineers to check it over and make sure that nothing has gone wrong?'

'Nothing is wrong with Psycho,' insisted Conway. He glared at the Chief of Genetics. 'If you ask me, it's you that is wrong, not Psycho. Maybe you'd better let Medical make certain that your 'highly-strung nerves' haven't sent you over the edge?'

'I don't have to listen to that kind of talk from you.' Malick jerked to his feet, his face red with anger. 'If you're a man at all, you'll meet me in the stadium!'

'Control yourself, Malick!' The Captain didn't raise his voice but something in the thin, penetrating tones chilled Malick's anger. 'You are overwrought or you would never have dared to challenge a fellow-member of the Council. Sit down and calm yourself.' He waited until Malick had resumed his seat, 'Now, let's look at this thing intelligently. You know perfectly well that all educational tapes are channeled from Psycho on automatic relay. No one could have touched them and, if what you say is true, then it must be as the builders intended. Are you questioning the wisdom of the builders?'

134

'No.' Malick looked uncomfortable. 'Of course not.'

'A pity. It is possible to place too great a reliance on the work of others.' Quentin stared down at his papers for a moment, then rose in dismissal. 'That will be all, gentlemen. I suggest that we each concentrate on our duties and waste no time in idle speculation.'

He stood by the head of the desk as they left the room, tall, proud, almost fatherly in the way he stared after them. Alone, he sat down and, closing his eyes, let his mind and thoughts mingle with the eternal, sub-audible vibration of the Ship which was his universe. It was happening again.

The same old distrust, intrigue, the playing for power and the breaking out of ambition. The envy, pride, jealousy and, above all, the mind-wrenching fear of what was to come. The hierarchy knew too much for their peace of mind. They were no longer young and, knowing what they did, they would fight against elimination with every weapon at their command. Quentin recognized it — had recognized it for some time now — and knew that in sheer self-defense if for no other reason he must protect himself. There was only one man in the Ship who was safe against the dictates of Psycho, and that man was the Captain.

Opening his eyes, he pressed a button on his desk and waited for the intercom to warm into life.

'Yes, sir?' His private aide. The one person he could trust in the entire Ship was someone unknown to the rest of the hierarchy and all the more valuable because of that. Quentin lowered his voice as he spoke into the instrument.

'Find Merrill and send him to me. Use caution.'

'Naturally, sir.'

The intercom died as the Captain broke the connection. He stared at it for a moment, his mind busy with plans; then, resting his head between his hands, he relaxed. His shoulders stooped, his muscles grew limp and flaccid, nerves and tendons sagged as he relaxed his iron control, and his breathing rasped in his throat as he sucked in great gasps of air.

In that moment he looked very old.

9

George was a long time arriving. Jay sat in a chair and stared moodily at the illuminated surface of the viewer screen, hardly noticing the images flashing before his eyes. Habit had made him switch on the viewer, the same, ingrained habit which made everyone in the Ship turn to education as the main form of amusement. But he found little to amuse him in the pictured representation of a dismantled radio set. He leaned forward and was about to switch it off when the door opened and George entered the room.

'Sorry to have kept you waiting, Jay. I got talking to another electronics man and forgot the time.

'Did you?' Jay turned the switch and watched the screen flicker and grow blank. 'What did you want to see me about, George?'

Curtway hesitated. Though he was older than Jay the difference was hardly noticeable; as they stood next to each other, they could have passed for brothers.

'It's about Susan,' he said awkwardly. 'I hardly know how to say this without causing offense, Jay, but I wish you wouldn't see her any more.'

'I see.' Jay looked at the elder man. 'You realize what you are saying, of course?'

'I mean no insult,' said George hastily. 'It's just that Susan is an impressionable girl and you're young and handsome. I'm not blaming you or anyone, Jay, but she's due for marriage soon and I don't want her to get into trouble with Genetics.'

'Are you accusing me of immorality?' Jay deliberately encouraged his mounting temper. George was making things very easy for him. An accusation like that was making things very easy for him. An accusation like that was sufficient ground for a challenge, and once he had George in the arena, the rest would be simple.

'No, Jay, you know that I wouldn't do that.'

'Then what objection can there be to my seeing her?'

'She's in love with you, Jay. That isn't good, not when there can't be any future in it for either of you. Unless you agree not to see her, you'll ruin her marriage and create discontent.' George stepped forward and rested his hand on the other's own. 'Be reasonable, Jay. I know that you're fond of Susan, but think of her own good. Later, when she's out of marriageable status, there'll be plenty of time for you to settle down together.'

'I don't like what you're saying, Curtway.' Jay shook off the hand on his arm. 'I consider that you've insulted me to an unpardonable extent. Naturally, you'll give me satisfaction.'

'No, Jay.'

'You refuse to fight?'

'Yes.' George glanced at the red dot on Jay's forearm. 'I'm no duelist, Jay, and I didn't think that you were either. If a father can't protect his daughter without fear of getting murdered by some arrogant bully, then there must be something wrong in the Ship. I don't think that you really mean what you say.'

'You have accused me of immorality,' said Jay coldly. 'I demand satisfaction.'

'You can't make me fight you, Jay.'

'You admit to being a coward, then?'

'I'll admit anything you like. Call me a waster if you want to. Hit me if it gives you any satisfaction, but I'm not going into the arena with you or any other man.' George smiled and deliberately sat down, 'Now, let's be sensible, Jay. I know you too well to believe that you would take advantage of an old man like that.'

He was right, of course, and Jay knew it. Nothing would persuade George to enter the arena and, despite his own urgency, Jay felt a little ashamed of trying to force a duel. Elimination should be quick, cold, utterly merciless and without mental or physical pain. To drag an old man into the arena and butcher him there for the benefit of the watchers was pure sadism. He sighed and joined George on the bench.

'All right, George. I can't make you fight if you don't want to.'

'And Susan?'

'I won't see her again if that's the way you want it.'

'It would be best, Jay.'

'All right, then. Forget it. The thing's over and done with.'

'Good.' George leaned forward to switch on the viewer, and Jay knew that it was time for him to go. He sat where he was.

'Was that all you wanted to see me about, George?'

'That's all. Thanks for waiting to see me — and the other thing.'

The other thing! Jay stared at the older man as he sat looking with interested at the moving picture on the screen. He could kill him now, a simple pressure on the carotids would do it, but killing wasn't enough. The death had to appear to be an accident and, glancing around the apartment, Jay knew that this was the wrong place.

'George.'

'Yes?' Curtway blinked as he turned from the screen.

'What is it, Jay?'

'I'm in trouble, George, and I wonder if

you could help me.'

'Trouble?'

'Yes. I was up near No-Weight a while ago, checking the ventilation tubes, and I spotted something I should have reported.' Jay shrugged. 'It slipped my mind during the fight and if I report it now I'll be down-graded for time-lag. It was in your department and I wondered . . . '

'Something to do with electronics?'

'That's right. One of those big, flat boxes — the ones with all the conduits leading from them. I noticed one smelled of burning and when I touched it I got a shock.'

'Probably a short due to condensation,' said George promptly. 'We've been having a lot of trouble with the junction boxes lately.' He looked at Jay. 'What do you want me to do?'

'I was hoping that you could fix it and save me trouble.' Jay made himself appear nervous. 'If it goes through normal channels I'll be slated for delay, and if I ignore it, they might even send me to sanitation. If you could fix it for me . . . '

'Up near No-Weight?' George frowned. 'Tell you what, Jay. I'll take a look at it, and if I can fix it, I will. Fair enough?'

'Thanks,' Jay said gratefully. He rose and stepped towards the door. 'Let's get it over with. I'm frightened someone else will spot it and report in.'

George sighed and followed him into the corridor.

As usual the area around No-Weight was deserted. Jay led the way among a tangle of girders, slipped into a narrow tube-like corridor, and paused by one of a number of junction boxes. George, maneuvering awkwardly in the almost total absence of weight, joined him.

'Is that the one?' He didn't look down at the box.

'I think so.' Jay stooped over it, touched it, then jerked back his hand as though he had received a shock. 'This is it, right enough. Take a look at it, George.'

'All right.' George kicked himself forward and, like most people unused to free fall, kicked too hard. Jay caught him as he passed and drew him to where George could grip a stanchion.

'Thanks.' The electronics man stooped over the box. 'Now let's see what the trouble is.'

He was wasting his time, of course, and Jay knew it. There was nothing wrong with the box at all, but it had served as a pretext to lure his victim to a place where his death could easily be accounted for. Looking at the man, Jay felt a strange reluctance to finish the job and, annoyed with himself for his hesitation, he moved in to make an end.

It would be simple. Pressure on the carotids, the great arteries of the throat leading to the brain, would bring swift unconsciousness; continued pressure would bring painless death. Jay knew just how to hold his victim so that any struggle would be useless. It would be routine, nothing more and, as he reached forward, he forced himself to ignore everything but his duty.

'Are you going to kill me, Jay?'

It wasn't so much what George said that shocked Jay into immobility, as the knowledge behind the words. He stood, swaying a little from the absence of gravity, and stared incredulously at the calm face of his intended victim.

'I've been expecting this,' continued George evenly. 'I guessed what you intended as soon as I saw the box. There's nothing wrong with it, and you know it.'

'You refused to fight,' stammered Jay desperately. He knew that at all costs he must keep the truth away from the other man. 'You insulted me.'

'That isn't why you wanted to kill me. Did Gregson send you?'

'Gregson?'

'Yes, Gregson, the head of psych-police.' George rested easily against the stanchion, his eyes serious as they stared at the young man. 'I'm not a fool, Jay, and I've suspected you for some time now. You worked at odd hours, seemed to be missing for long periods of time and didn't appear to have any particular duties.' George shrugged. 'I wouldn't have noticed it, I suppose, but for your attachment to Susan. I couldn't understand why, if you were young enough, you weren't married. That made me wonder. The final proof came when I saw you at headquarters one shift.'

'You saw me there?'

'Yes. I had been to service Psycho — I'm a top-line electronic engineer, you know, and they trust me to service the machine. I took a short cut back to sector five and passed P.P. headquarters. I saw you there — and you weren't wearing red shorts!'

'*You fool!*' Jay shifted his grip on the girder next to him in readiness for a lunge at the other man. 'Don't you realize that you've signed your own death warrant?'

'Gregson did that for me a long time ago.' George stared contemptuously at the young man. 'Don't try anything, Jay. I'm ready and warned and I've had practice in free fall.' He shifted as he spoke and Jay could see that his previous awkwardness had been assumed.

'Listen, George,' he said desperately. 'Let's be reasonable about this. There's nothing personal about it, you know that, but I've got to kill you. If I don't, then I'll be eliminated for failure of duty.'

'Do you know why you were ordered to kill me, Jay?'

146

'No.'

'Then I'll tell you. I found out something about Gregson. I tried to get a private interview with the Captain to tell him what I'd learned but he refused to see me. Gregson knows now that I know what he did. To safeguard himself he has ordered my death. That's the truth of the matter, Jay. Do you still want to kill me?'

'I must. Believe me, George I'd rather do anything than eliminate you, but the welfare of the Ship depends on it. You don't understand.'

'I understand well enough, Jay. I told you that I was no fool, and I've eyes to see with and a mind to think with, and a brain to correlate the resultant data. I know, for example, that there is no natural death aboard the Ship.'

'You're wrong,' insisted Jay sickly. 'People die in Medical.'

'They die, yes, but from what? Injections, perhaps? Wounds received in the arena? How many people have died of old age, Jay? Can you answer that?'

Jay could, but he didn't dare. The answer was that not one person had ever died of old age. They had never been allowed to live that long. 'Accidents,' duels, strange relapses: all had accounted for every death since the Ship had left Earth so long ago. Senility, white hair, doddering men and women were incomprehensible to the Ship's personnel. Old age was something which just didn't exist.

'If you live,' said Jay thickly, 'you will be robbing a newborn child of its air and water, living-space and food.' He moved a little nearer to the older man. 'You've had your time, George. Now you must die so that others can have their chance of life.'

'I don't mind dying,' said George calmly. 'I'm intelligent enough to realize the necessity, and life isn't so wonderful that I should want to cling to its every moment. But is it fair that I should die while others cheat their turn?'

'Cheat? What do you mean?' The accusation shocked Jay even more than Curtway's knowledge of what he was and what he did. 'How could anyone cheat?'

'There is a way, if you're in the right position to manage it. Gregson is in that position, Jay. I know what he did and he knows that I know.' George took a step forward. 'Can't you see the danger, Jay? If one man can avoid his turn for death, then so can others. How long will it be before the Ship is a despotism ruled by a handful of old men?'

And that was the trouble. While elimination was fair for all, then no intelligent person could argue against his turn. Not that they were given the choice. No one could be expected to remain wholly sane while he lived from day to day in anticipation of a death hour decided before his birth. Such knowledge would disrupt the routine of the Ship and convert its smooth-running system into a shambles. The old would demand rigid birth control so that they could live a little longer. The young would be frustrated at the thwarting of their natural desire for children. A gap would arise between the generations with the resultant loss of sympathy between age and youth. Such a system would lead to racial sterility, degeneration, and collapse of moral fiber.

This was why the psych-police were among the most carefully selected personnel on board, trained and indoctrinated from early youth to accept the twin burdens of responsibility and silence. But if what they had been taught was a lie?

'You're wrong,' insisted Jay desperately. 'No one would be so immoral as to cheat like that.'

'You think not?' George shrugged. 'I'm an old man, Jay, and to the old life becomes a precious thing. To you death is something utterly remote, even though you know full well that one day someone will eliminate you as you tried to eliminate me. But when you get older you sense things. You have more time for thought and you begin to realize all the things that you've missed in life. You want to hang on, Jay. You want to cling to life as a newlywed wants to cling to his bride, or as a mother to her first-born. You can't be logical then. You can't evaluate and accept what must be. No. You want to live — and you'd do anything for a few extra years of existence.'

'Gregson is old,' said Jay thoughtfully. 'I

hadn't realized it before.'

'Gregson is afraid of death,' said George. 'I know that.' He took another step forward and touched Jay on the arm. 'What are you going to do, Jay?'

'I don't know. I've orders and you know what they are — but if what you say is true . . . '

'It's true.'

'Then you must see the Captain.'

'How?' George shrugged with unusual cynicism. 'I've already tried to get a private interview with the Captain. My request was refused. To try again I must pass my request through the psych-police. I'm supposed to be dead. If I make the application then Gregson will set his dogs on me again.' He looked at Jay. 'Can you suggest something?'

'I don't know,' said Jay miserably. 'Obviously you'll have to hide until a chance comes for you to see the Captain. If Gregson ever finds out I've failed to eliminate you, he'll order my own death for inefficiency, so in order to cover up, I'll have to fake your accidental death.' He bit his lips in indecision. 'You could hide out in No-Weight. I can smuggle you past the guard, but the accident — '

'How did you intend explaining my death?'

'Simple. I was going to kill you and then dash your head against a stanchion. The official verdict would have been that you had misjudged your speed and distance and crushed your skull on landing.' Jay shrugged. 'That idea's no good now. Merrill will investigate and, unless your 'body' is unrecognizable, he will guess at what I've done.' Jay held out his hand. 'Give me your identity disc and shorts.'

'Why? What are you going to do?'

'I don't know yet, but I'll think of something.' Jay snapped his fingers with impatience. 'Hurry.'

Reluctantly, George stripped off his blue shorts and struggled to remove the stamped metal identity tag from his wrist. He swore as he scraped skin from his knuckles, but he finally managed to get it off. He handed it to Jay.

'Now what?'

'Now you hide in No-Weight. I'll try to

smuggle you up some food and water but don't worry if I don't come for a while. You won't stay there long, anyway. The quicker I can arrange an interview with the Captain the better.'

Silently Jay led the way along the winding tube, drifting lightly from stanchion to stanchion, pausing just long enough to impel himself in a new direction, twisting his body with expert ease to cushion the shock of landing with his knees and thighs. Finally he paused at a sunken panel.

'This is an emergency entry into No-Weight. It's kept locked from this side and I'll have to fasten it behind you.' Jay spun a wheel and jerked the metal slab open. 'Right, George. In you go. Try to stay close to the panel if you can. When I bring you supplies I don't want to have to waste a lot of time.'

'I understand.' George stepped towards the opening and peered into the dark interior. He shivered a little. 'It's cold in there.'

'The converters are colder,' snapped Jay impatiently.

George nodded and stepped through the opening into the vast cavern of No-Weight. He caught hold of the edge of the door and looked at Jay, his head a pale blob against the darkness behind him.

'What about Susan?'

'Susan will believe that you are dead.' Jay glanced uneasily down the corridor. 'To her, as to everyone, you will have met with an unfortunate accident.' He softened as he swung shut the door. 'I'm sorry, George, but there's nothing else I can do.'

'No,' said George slowly. 'I suppose not.' He hesitated. 'Still, I'd have liked to say goodbye. Funny, that . . . no one ever thinks of it until it's too late to do anything about it.' He removed his hand from the edge of the opening. 'Take care of her, Jay. And thank you.'

Jay didn't answer. He was already spinning shut the locking wheel.

10

Merrill was afraid of the Captain. He stood before the wide desk, acutely conscious of the old man's scrutiny, and tried to assume an arrogance and recklessness he did not feel. Quentin smiled a little as he saw it, the tolerant, almost amused smile of conscious superiority, but he did not speak, just stared and allowed Merrill to feel the mounting tension. It was one of the oldest psychological tricks known, so old that it always worked. Merrill spoke first.

'You sent for me, sir.'

'Are you ambitious?'

'I . . .' Merrill blinked at the unexpectedness of the question, then, as he recovered, his eyes grew wary. 'Yes, sir. I suppose that I am. Every man likes to do the best he can for the welfare of the Ship and . . .'

'You like to control men,' interrupted Quentin and his voice held a subtle contempt at Merrill's protestations. 'You enjoy the feel of power, the knowledge that you, even in a small part, control destiny.' He leaned a little forward over the desk. 'Tell me, do you like to kill?'

'I am efficient.'

'Then you enjoy what you do.' Quentin smiled and relaxed against the back of his chair. 'Don't bother to lie to me, Merrill. I know more about you than you know yourself. You may know what you do and think that knowledge is sufficient. But I know why you do what you do, and that knowledge makes me your master.' He let his thin voice fade into silence and his eyes grew bleak and distant. 'Remember that, Merrill. Always remember it. I am your master. The moment you forget that — you die.'

There was no passion in the thin tones, no arrogance or self-convincing bluster-ing. It was a cold statement of fact and, hearing it, Merrill swallowed.

'Yes, sir. I understand.'

'Good.' Quentin smiled for the first time. 'Now to business. I have sent for you because, though you may not know it, I have studied you for several years now and have decided that you are the man I need. Men grow old, Merrill, and you know what happens to them when age piles its weight of invisible years on their heads. Some men accept their fate, others . . . '

'Gregson,' said Merrill, and stiffened in sudden fear. Quentin smiled.

'I knew that you were intelligent,' he said softly. 'But try not to be *too* intelligent.' He leaned forward again, his elbows on the desk, his thin fingers caressing his throat. 'We need mention no names and we need leap to no assumptions. I want a tool, nothing more, and a tool must be willing to obey without question or hesitation the dictates of its user. A time will come, maybe soon, maybe not so soon, when a job will have to be done. A man will have reached the end of his allotted span and, knowing that man, he may not be willing to yield his life and position. In such a case a tool must be used, a dumb, willing, obedient tool.' The old man looked at Merrill. 'You understand?'

'I do.'

'Men are ambitious,' said Quentin, speaking more to himself than to the man standing opposite him. 'Sometimes ambition can be dangerous, not only to them, but to those around them. Promises could be made and glittering prizes offered if . . . But there is only one man aboard the Ship who can really offer anything other than empty dreams. I am that man. Do as I say and you will have what you have won. Disobey me and . . . ' He shrugged and looked directly at Merrill. 'A wise man has many tools and relies on none. I trust that I have made myself clear?'

'Perfectly.' Merrill tried not to smile at the prospects before him. 'When?'

'I will tell you when. Until then you will obey your orders, say nothing, think nothing, and, above all, do nothing.' Quentin rose in dismissal. 'You may go.'

He watched the young man stride from the room, his departing back radiating his arrogance and anticipation of what was to come and, watching him, Quentin felt pity for his blindness. Merrill was a killer, nothing more, and his usefulness ended there.

But he didn't know that.

From the bridge, Merrill was conducted down a hidden passageway towards his own sector, and he walked the droning corridors with his mind full of what he had just heard. The old man wanted him to stand ready to eliminate Gregson. That was obvious, and equally obvious was the fact that he would take over as chief of psych-police. Merrill smiled as he thought about it. The job itself was worth having with its attached privileges of private rooms, a seat on the Council, and literal life and death power over every man and woman in the Ship. But it meant more than that. Once in power Merrill intended to stay there and, knowing what he knew of the system the Captain apparently used, he would make certain that no one ever took over his job.

Two could play at the game of assassination.

He was still living in a world of his imagination when he felt a hand on his arm and turned to stare at the sullen features of Sam Aldway.

'What do you want?'

'I want to talk with you.' Sam glanced over his shoulder. 'Let's go somewhere private.'

Merrill hesitated for a moment, then led the way to a common rec-room. Closing the door behind them, he tripped the 'engaged' signal and glared at Aldway.

'Well?'

'I took him into the arena,' muttered Sam. 'You know who I mean.'

'So he agreed to fight?' Merrill smiled. 'Good. I never thought that he would. You killed him, of course.'

'No.'

'No?'

'I didn't kill him — in fact he almost killed me.' Sam fingered his bruised throat. 'Even now I don't know just what he did. I had him, another minute and he'd have been ready for the converters, and then the lights went out and the next thing I knew the attendant was standing over me.' He winced as he touched the transparent plastic over his eye and lip. 'You should have told me that he was up on all the tricks. Hell! I thought that he was just a neo.'

'Would I have trained you in that case?' Merrill stared at the man with undisguised contempt. 'So you failed. For all your boasting you let a first-timer beat you up and make a fool out of you.' He shrugged. 'Well, you've had your chance.'

'Wait a minute!' Sam grabbed at Merrill's arm as he stepped towards the door, then yelped as a stiffened hand slashed at the inside of his elbow.

'Keep your paws off me,' Merrill glared at the hydroponics worker as if he could have killed him. 'How dare you touch me!'

'I'm sorry.' Sam massaged his tingling arm.

'What about that job you promised me?'

'I promised you nothing. I merely told you that I couldn't have two assistants at the same time, but even that doesn't matter now. You've had your chance and failed. I've no time or patience with failures.' Merrill stepped towards the door and stood, his hand on the latch, looking at the other man. 'Forget it Aldway. Stay at your job and keep out of trouble. I can't help you now.'

'Wait!' Sam stared desperately at the cold face of the officer. 'I can try again.'

'He'll never let you get him into the stadium a second time. Even if you did, he would beat you just as he did before, and this time he might kill you in order to get rid of a nuisance.' Merrill lifted the latch. 'Sorry, Sam, better take my advice and forget it.'

'I can't.' Sam looked ill as he thought about it. 'I can't spend the rest of my life tending those damn plants. I won't do it.' He stepped forward, his eyes appealing. 'Look, supposing he dies. Never mind how, but supposing he does. Would I get his job?

'Maybe.' Merrill pretended to think about it. 'Unless of course, you were arrested for murder and sent to the converters.'

'I'll take that chance,' said Sam eagerly. 'Well?'

'If he dies,' said Merrill slowly, 'I'll be needing a new assistant. He opened the door. 'It's up to you, Sam. It's all up to you.' The door closed behind him and Sam smiled.

It wasn't a nice smile.

He sat in the room for a while, his mind busy with unaccustomed thoughts. To kill was easy, or so he had always thought, but to get away with it was the important thing. The alternative was the converters or, if he took Merrill's advice, a lifetime of manual labor in the farm. Thinking about it made him feel sick, and as he blamed Jay for his position, he began to hate where before he had only been contemptuous. By the time he left the room he was boiling with rage and almost frenzied in his desire to kill the man who stood between him and his ambition.

A couple passed him as he entered the corridor, both fully mature, the woman wearing the dull beige of the kitchens and the man the gray of waste reclamation. The woman stared at him and moved towards the vacated room. The man glanced at Sam's passion-distorted features and laughed before following the woman into the rec-room.

Sam paused, his hands knotting at his sides, fighting the desire to hammer on the door until it opened and then to smash the laughing face into pulp. He tried to control himself. There would be time enough for vengeance later, more time than he would need, and the training which Merrill would give him would make victory all the easier. But first he had a job to do.

He went looking for Jay.

He found him in one of the passages leading down from the upper levels and, cursing the people thronging the crowded corridor, began to stalk his victim like the blood-crazed beast he was. Instinctively he took care that he should not be seen and, with an effort of will, managed to control his features so that to a casual watcher he would appear to be intent on his own business. His experience in the arena had taught him that the young man was dangerous, too dangerous for fair fight, and as he followed the figure in the red shorts, Sam began running over the tricks Merrill had taught him.

Jay was totally unaware of the man behind him. He had his own worries and, as he turned from the busy passage into a quieter, more deserted region, he began to regret having helped George escape to No-Weight. It had been easy to talk of plans but carrying them out was something else. He frowned as he touched the folded blue shorts beneath his own red ones and his eyes, as he walked along, were never still. He had to find a man to take Curtway's place. Had, in effect, to murder an innocent stranger so that someone could snatch a few more weeks of life. At first he had viewed the scheme with cold detachment but, as time passed, he felt a growing reluctance to do what was necessary.

Operating under orders from P.P. headquarters was one thing, but acting as a freelance was something quite different: In the first case he had no responsibility, no feeling of guilt or shame and he could take a quiet pride in an effective elimination as a job done efficiently and well. But now? He gritted his teeth as he tried to overcome his indoctrination and select a body with which to stage the 'accident.'

He paused before the door of Curt-way's cubicle, saw by the external sign that it was empty, and walked inside. It would be better to have the body discovered in its own quarters; it would help identification for one thing, and for another it gave him time to set the stage for the 'accident' which must almost completely destroy the body. In all the Ship, the only way to do that was by electrocution, and grimly Jay squatted down beside a masking plate and began to undo the fastenings.

He barely heard the soft whisper of feet behind him as Sam lunged to the attack.

He half-turned just in time to avoid the full impact of the blow intended to snap his vertebrae but even then the side of his neck went numb and darkness flooded his vision. Desperately he staggered to his feet, automatically twisting to avoid the knee thrust at his groin, and tasted blood as fingers stabbed at his throat. Again the searing, nerve-paralyzing blows tore at his consciousness, sapping his strength and dimming his reflexes, so that he reeled helplessly against the metal wall, the hard surface bruising his cheek.

He could have died then, would have died if Sam had remained cool, but science yielded to frenzied instinct and Sam forgot what he had been taught. Instead of standing back and hitting with calculated precision, he tried to hit too often and too fast. He slashed at barely seen targets, stabbed at spots not quite as vulnerable as others, beat with savage but stupid energy at bone and muscle. He caused pain, the sickening pain of torn muscle and jarred nerve but, because of that very pain, he defeated his own ends.

Jay, spurred by his pain, shook off his numbness and fought back.

He was smooth and deliberate, the expert against the amateur, the professional assassin against the would-be murderer. Sam never stood a chance and when it was all over, Jay was still only half-aware of what he had done. He leaned against the wall, mechanically massaging his tormented neck; then, as he stared at the dead man at his feet, he smiled for the first time since receiving his assignment.

The door was closed and the signal which would prevent anyone from violating the advertised privacy was in place. Quickly Jay stripped the brown shorts from the dead man and exchanged them for the blue ones he had taken from Curtway. The identity disc was a harder job, and he sweated as he dragged it from the limp wrist and replaced it with the other. That done, he stooped over the masking plate and removed it from the wall, standing it against the bench before returning to peer into the revealed cavity.

Wires ran thick and heavy behind the metal of the wall. The triple circuits of the Ship, some for power, some for light, still others for the emergency illumination never used and now only assumed to be in existence. Jay frowned at them, wondering which would be the best for his purpose; then, as he remembered another, similar case, shrugged and dragged the dead body towards the opening.

It would be a sloppy job. No electronics

man in his right mind would ever allow himself to be electrocuted, and George was an expert in his trade. For a moment Jay hesitated, pride of workmanship struggling against sheer necessity; then, thrusting forward the limp, right hand, he let it fall on to the wires.

The stench was awful. It was a blend of ozone and burnt blood, of charred flesh and seared metal. It was nauseating, vile and, as blue lightning tore across the widening gap between flesh and metal, Jay fought against the desire to vomit. He swallowed, desperately trying to quell his sickness, and stared at the blackened shape lying before him.

It had been human, male, had worn blue shorts and still carried a scrap of metal around his left wrist. That was all that could be told. Satisfied, Jay rose to his feet and stepped towards the door. Somewhere a fuse would have blown and meters kicked. Watchers would report a power-drop and men would be sent out to investigate. They would find a dead men and an exposed wire. They would report it to Merrill who, because of his job, would state that the entire occurrence had been an accident. The men in olive would come to collect the remains, other men would repair the damage, and the thing would be over and forgotten.

Except for Susan's tears.

She would believe her father dead, but there could be no help for that. There could be no comfort, no whispered reassurances, no betrayal of what had really happened. George Curtway was officially dead — and Jay's life depended on everyone believing that.

He stepped out into the corridor, closing the door behind him, and strode along the passage. He felt dirty and his stomach heaved when he remembered odor of roasting meat. It seemed to be all around him, to have permeated the very pores of his skin, to cling to his hair and shorts. He wanted to strip and step into a shower, to lather his body and wash away the stench, to stare at an educational tape and cleanse his mind. He didn't notice Susan until he bumped into her.

'Jay!' For a moment she clung to him; then, remembering their last parting, moved consciously away. 'Sorry, but it was really your fault.'

'Forget it.' He stared down at her. 'Where are you going?'

'To see Dad.' She attempted to move past him. 'Please let me pass, Jay.'

'No.' He took her arm and tried to make her walk with him. 'Let's go and watch a tape or something. I haven't seen you for — '

'Please!' Coldly she removed his hand, her nose crinkling as if she smelled an unfamiliar scent. 'You seem to have a bad memory, Jay. I haven't.'

Numbly he watched her walk away from him down the passage towards her father's cubicle. He wanted to stop her, to force her to come with him, to do anything to prevent her from seeing that sight. But there was nothing he could do. Nothing.

He heard her scream as he left the corridor.

11

Gregson stood and watched the machine of destiny. It was big, as it had to be to hold all the filed information, the various educational tapes, the selective master-plates, the cards, the erasers and computers. In itself it was a master-piece of planning, constructed by the builders centuries ago to serve as a guide and a master above and beyond all limitations of human flesh. The Ship could forget its purpose, the personnel waste themselves in ambition and selfish pleasure, the race sicken and die from stupidity and greed, but Psycho would always be ready to give the information to restore the essential balance if the project of which it was a part was to succeed.

And yet it was not wholly omnipotent It could advise but it still needed the human touch to transform its dictates into action. Looking at it, Gregson felt a quiet pride in being one of the few elect. He turned as Conway came towards him.

The psychologist carried a thin sheaf of plastic cards, rejects from the file banks, now erased and ready for further duty. He dumped them into a hopper, threw a lever, and smiled as a man who sees the completion of a job well done.

'Fascinating, isn't it, Gregson?' Conway rested his hand on the metal casing of the machine. 'Just think, inside there are the full details of every man and woman, child and newborn babe aboard the Ship. Every tiny detail, fed in fragment by fragment from Medical, Genetics, Supply, the Kitchens, the observers, all correlated and intermeshed by Psycho into a composite whole so that, at any moment, we can determine the efficiency rating of anyone we wish.'

'Anyone?' Gregson's expression matched the dryness of his tones. 'The Captain?'

'Not the Captain, at least I don't think so.' Conway looked disturbed. 'He can't be, can he?'

'Not at his age he can't.'

'Well, then, everyone except the Captain.' Conway caressed the machine again. 'The more you think about it, the more wonderful Psycho becomes. It selects and channels the educational tapes, determines the exact amount of all material aboard, maintains the temperature and humidity of the air, keeps — '

'It's a machine,' interrupted Gregson harshly. 'Nothing more than an elaborate electronic device. Stop talking about it as though it was a god.'

'I trust Psycho,' said Conway mechanically. He looked over his shoulder at where an assistant worked at a desk, and lowered his voice. 'Control yourself, Gregson. We may be observed.'

'Quentin is no god either.' Gregson stared at the smooth bulk of Psycho as though it were a human enemy. 'He is an old man, too old.'

'He's still the Captain.'

'There were other Captains before Quentin,' said Gregson deliberately, 'and there will be others after him. How long must we let him live before making a change?'

'Are you insane!' Conway stepped forward, his eyes fearful as he stared around him. 'If he should learn of this . . . '

'Why should he?' Gregson shrugged but when he spoke again it was almost a whisper. 'Relax, Conway. We're alone now and there's no need for us to pretend to each other. Is Quentin's card in Psycho?'

'I don't know. He's the only person in the Ship who doesn't wear an identity disc. His card may be filed with the others, but how can I tell? Without his number it would be impossible to find.'

'It isn't in there, then,' said Gregson with quiet certainty. 'The first thing any Captain with sense would do to remove it. Quentin is no fool, he wouldn't be the Captain if he were, and no fool would have managed to stay alive so long.' His eyes as he stared at Conway held a sick envy. 'How old would you say he is, Conway?'

'Thirteenth generation?' The psychologist shrugged. 'I don't know. How is an old man supposed to look, Gregson? I've never seen one to base an estimate on.

Quentin could be thirteenth or even twelfth, but I'm only guessing.'

'Say thirteenth,' whispered Gregson. 'That would make him anything between seventy-seven and fifty-eight years old.' He licked his lips. 'Twelfth? Twenty years more? Is it possible, Conway? Could a man live almost a hundred years?'

'Impossible!'

'Are you sure?'

'No, I'm not sure,' snapped the psychologist irritably. 'How could I be? But the thing is against all logic. You heard what Malick said: a man's usefulness ends once he has fathered the new generation, and we know that Psycho determines the life expectancy at around forty years. The builders set that figure, and the builders knew what they were doing. After forty a man's efficiency begins to fail. Can you imagine what state a man would be in if, by some miracle, he managed to live so long? The concept is ludicrous.'

'Perhaps you're right.' Gregson seemed reluctant to dismiss the idea. 'Put it at seventy then, or even sixty. That's still twenty years beyond the normal expectancy. A full generation!'

'For the Captain only,' reminded Conway. 'The rest of us still wear our discs and our cards are still filed in Psycho.'

'Yes.' Gregson stared at the humped bulk of the machine. 'Of course. And at any time those cards could be sorted, rejected, expelled and sent down to me.' He looked at Conway. 'To the executioner.'

'I know it.' Conway shuddered at an unpleasant memory. 'Every time I threw the trip-lever to expel the latest batch, I wondered whether or not my card would be among them. Sometimes I couldn't stand the strain and had to call an assistant to take over.'

'But not now.'

'No.' Conway glanced at Gregson as a dog might lick its master's hand. 'You ended that nightmare.'

'Postponed it,' corrected the chief of psych-police. 'We still wear our discs and are still vulnerable to questions. Both of us are fourteenth generation. Neither of us is young. Others are watching us — my officers, your assistants, even the Captain. One day someone is going to ask some pertinent questions and when they do . . . '

He shrugged.

'You'll take care of that,' stammered Conway. 'You took care of the other thing, didn't you?'

'I showed you what to do and you did it. Anyone but a fool would have thought of it for himself, but, even if you had, you would still have needed me as I needed you.' Gregson rested his hand on the machine. 'Even at that we were discovered. An electronics engineer stumbled on something and requested an interview with the Captain.'

'I remember that.' Conway looked troubled. 'What's going to happen?'

'Nothing, the man is dead.' Gregson smiled with conscious power. 'Didn't you expel his card for me. What else could I do but order his elimination?'

'So we're safe then.' Conway sagged with relief. 'Good. For a moment there you had me worried, Gregson, but with you controlling the police and with me in charge of Psycho, nothing can go wrong.' He frowned. 'I wish I could find out what it was that man discovered. If he found it, then others could.'

'Forget it. He's dead and, if others ask too many questions, they will die also.' Gregson glanced around to make sure that they weren't overheard. 'Our biggest danger is Quentin. I don't like the way he stares at me and I've the feeling he's up to something. I think that it's time we moved in.'

'Mutiny?' Conway shook his head. 'No, Gregson. I won't stand for that.'

'Who said anything about mutiny? Quentin is old, and old men die . . . it happens all the time. If Quentin died, then we'd have to appoint a new Captain. The only problem we have to face is who? Not Henderly, not Folden, and certainly not Malick. The man's almost insane as it is with his babble about tapes showing meat eating. You? How long would you last alone? No, Conway, *I'm* going to be the next Captain. Help me and your life is secure. Oppose me and I'll have to arrange an 'accident'.'

'I won't oppose you, but I won't help you mutiny either.' Conway spoke with a lifetime of indoctrination against the concept of forcible overthrow of authority. 'If Quentin should die, that's different. I'll stand by you as the new Captain.'

'Yes,' said Gregson dryly. 'After all, there's nothing else you can do, is there? As Captain I'd be the one man in the Ship to safeguard your secret.' He stepped away as the assistant, apparently finishing his task, rose from his desk and came towards them.

'Well, Conway,' he said for the other's benefit. 'Give me the cards and let me get on with the eliminations, I've still got the Barb problem to worry about.'

'Any fresh news on that?' Conway nodded to his assistant and reached for a lever, one of many on a panel before him. 'Maybe it would be as well to let them alone, If Henderly is right — '

'Henderly is a fool. He underrates the danger of starving men. He talks of cannibalism, and forgets that meat eating is unthinkable to any normal person.' His face darkened and he leaned forward as the psychologist tripped the lever. 'I wonder how many this time?'

'Can't tell.' Conway stepped beside him as he stared at the disposal tray. 'The whole operation is automatic. Psycho is scanning the cards now for any which do not fit into the pre-selected master pattern. All unfit will be rejected.' His voice warmed as he waited for the machine to finish its task. 'It's really wonderful, you know, Gregson. It's like building a new race on a previously determined matrix. Eliminate the unfit and save the essentials.'

'Then we must have a perfect race,' said Gregson dryly as he looked at the empty tray. 'No rejects?'

'Not as many as there have been,' admitted Conway. 'I don't understand it, but Psycho can't be wrong.' He smiled as two cards fell into the tray. 'Two out of five thousand. Here.' He picked up the cards, scanned them, and passed them to Gregson. 'A woman, Julia Connors, sanitation, sector Four and a man, Sam

Aldway, hydroponics, sector five,'

'Again?' Gregson glanced casually at the cards. 'Sector five seems to be getting more than its fair share of eliminations recently.' He shrugged. 'We should worry, just so long as it isn't us, eh?' He laughed and, after a moment, Conway and the assistant laughed with him.

The assistant was the only one not genuinely amused. Aside from the communications man and Carter, the stand-by officer, headquarters was empty when Gregson returned. While waiting for Jay to answer his code signal he leaned back and, in the privacy of his office, surveyed his plans. Conway had been useful, might still be of some assistance, but, because of what he knew, would have to be eliminated as soon as Gregson had achieved his ambition. Malick too, the geneticist, was obviously irrational and, unless controlled, might cause later trouble. Henderly and Folden could continue on the Council for awhile, but Conway would certainly have to be disposed of.

Merrill, too.

Gregson was ambitious enough to take risks, but not fool enough to be blind to the ambitions of others. Merrill was untrustworthy and a defense would have to be found against him. No man could rule longer than his companions allowed him and, with ambitious men, any rule would seem too long. Gregson sat in his chair and hooded his eyes as he thought of the Captain.

Quentin was an old, senile fool — or was he? To the young all old men are fools, for the young insist on mistaking caution for fear, cool thinking for stupidity, tolerance for weakness. Quentin was old, fantastically old, sixty at least and maybe more, and he had been Captain for as long as Gregson could remember. But did mere age automatically qualify him for stupidity? Gregson sighed as he thought about it, then sat upright as Jay entered the office.

'You sent for me?' Jay looked tired. He had managed to get a shower but still felt unclean. He doubted whether a full soaking for a good ten minutes would serve to wash away the lingering traces of the odor surrounding him.

'Yes.' Gregson picked up the assignment card and threw it towards the officer. 'Another job in your sector. The other one completed yet?'

'Yes.' Jay stared numbly at the card and managed to control his instinctive reaction. Sam Aldway! The man he had planted to replace Curtway's missing body. The problem, instead of being solved, had only been postponed. He still had to find and eliminate an innocent stranger and, for a moment, he had a nightmare of continual assignments, each for the man he had just killed. He became aware of Gregson's eyes.

'Something wrong?'

'No.' Jay returned the assignment card to the desk. 'Why do you ask?'

'You looked odd. Sorry to keep you so busy but you know how these things are. They average out and you'll probably be bored to tears during the next few months.'

'You think so?' Jay didn't respond to the friendliness in the other's voice.

'I'm sure of it. I remember one time when . . . '

Gregson broke off as the door opened and Merrill entered the office. 'What do you want? Didn't they tell you that I was engaged?'

'They did, but it can't wait.' Merrill smiled with secret knowledge and stared at Jay. 'You'd better change. You look better in red shorts.'

'Change?' Jay felt his stomach tighten with apprehension. 'Why? What's wrong?'

'You'll find out.'

Jay hesitated then, at Gregson's curt nod, reversed his black shorts and donned them red side outwards. Merrill watched him, a faint grin of triumph lurking at the corners of his mouth, then jerked his thumb towards the door.

'Outside. There's someone out there who wants to see you.'

'Hold it a second.' Gregson stepped from behind his desk. 'I give the orders, Merrill. Now, what's wrong?'

'Ask Jay.'

'I asked you,' snapped Gregson impatiently. 'Don't get too big for yourself,

Merrill. I suggest that you remember a conversation we had a short while ago.'

'I'm remembering,' Merrill didn't trouble to hide his enjoyment. 'That's what makes this so sweet. Jay's bungled a job and managed to do it perfectly. He not only electrocuted an electronics engineer, in itself so stupid as to be incredible, but he did the job in the man's own cubicle and before a witness. I received the official complaint even before I had viewed the body. Name, time, place — everything.' He smiled at Jay. 'You must have really been trying.'

'Shut up!' Gregson bit at his lower lip. 'Did you bring the witness in quietly?'

'Quietly?' Merrill shrugged. 'She was in the center of a crowd when I arrived. Her brother, who is also an electronics man, was with her and about a couple of dozen others. They all heard her name the accused and make the official complaint. Her brother swore that he'd make it his business to see that the killer was brought to justice. Get rid of the witness and you'll have every electronics man in the Ship asking questions, let alone trouble with Genetics for disposing of a marriage-able female.'

'Waste!' Gregson glared at Merrill's smiling face. 'Fetch the witness. And wipe that grin off your face too — this is a serious matter.' He stared at Jay. 'Curt-way?'

'Yes.'

'Is Merrill telling the truth?'

'I don't know,' said Jay miserably. 'I had to rush the job, that part is true, but — '

'But the man is dead?'

'Yes.'

'I see,' Gregson stood for a moment, his face bleak with thought. 'You were a fool, West,' he said dispassionately, 'but maybe we can manage to settle this. Did the girl actually see you eliminate the man?'

'Of course not.'

'Good.' Gregson turned towards the door as Merrill, accompanied by a woman, entered the inner office. 'My officer informs me that you wish to make an accusation,' he rapped. 'Is that correct?'

'It is.' Susan stared with tear-swollen

eyes directly towards Jay. 'There he is. That is the man who killed my father.' She pointed towards him and Jay could almost feel her radiated scorn and hatred. 'I accuse that man of murder and demand the full punishment as laid down in the Ship's Code!'

The full punishment was agonizing death.

12

For a long moment no one moved or spoke. Finally, as Susan let her arm fall to her side and bowed her head, Gregson stepped behind his desk and sat down.

'Let us have some self-control here,' he said coldly. 'Merrill, if the girl can't stop crying take her out until she can. This office is not the place for tears.'

The very harshness of his voice produced the desired result. Susan dabbed at her eyes, lifted her head, and allowed Merrill to seat her in a chair. Gregson gestured for Jay to seat himself and looked at Merrill.

'Report.'

'I was notified of a power drop by electronics and went to the cubicle at fault. On arrival I was accosted by this young woman who accused a certain ventilation engineer named Jay West of the murder of her father. On investigation I found within the cubicle the body of a man, wearing the identity disc of George Curtway and the blue shorts of an electronic engineer. The man had died from electrocution.'

'I see.' Gregson stared at Susan. 'You realize, of course, the seriousness of this accusation. Murder, together with mutiny and waste, is a crime punishable by death. In the ease of wanted, premeditated murder together with mutiny, the death penalty also carries the punishment of torture.' He paused. 'I mention this so that you may be aware of the gravity of the charge.'

'I hope they make him scream for years,' said Susan viciously. 'He killed my father.' She did not look at Jay. Gregson sighed.

'You actually saw the crime committed?'

'Of course not,' she snapped. 'Would I have stood by and watched my father being murdered?'

'Then what makes you so certain that this man is the guilty party?' Gregson glanced at Merrill. 'How old was the deceased?'

'Fourteenth generation,' said Merrill easily. 'He was an expert electronic engineer.'

'I asked you his age, not his capabilities.' Gregson softened his voice as he spoke to the girl. 'You see? Your father was an old man, my dear, and old men aren't always predictable. There is no proof that anyone killed him at all.'

'He's dead, isn't he?'

'Of course, but the death could have been accidental.'

'No.'

'You can't be sure of that,' insisted Gregson gently. 'We of the psych-police, perhaps better than anyone else, know how soon a man can lose his mental stability when he nears his fortieth year. Perhaps your father felt his coming decline and, though I hesitate to suggest it, he may have decided to terminate his own life.'

'Ridiculous!' Susan shifted angrily in her chair and glared her contempt at the suggestion. 'My father would never have committed suicide.'

'How can you be certain of that?'

Gregson stared down at the surface of his desk then looked directly at the girl. 'The very method of death is . . . suggestive, don't you think? Who better than an expert in electronics would know just where the heavy current cables were to be found? Such a man would know how quick and painless death from electrocution would be. It seems logical to assume that your father may have chosen that way to end his life.'

'My father was sane,' stated Susan flatly. 'He was as efficient and as capable as he had ever been. He was old, true, but not that old. He was murdered.'

Looking at her, Jay had to admire her spirit. She knew nothing of the policy of the psych-police, naturally, and to her Gregson must seem a tedious old man trying to avoid the issue so that he could save himself work. Skillful handling by Merrill could have saved the situation but, glancing at the officer, Jay knew that, even if Susan hadn't made the accusation, she would have been encouraged into it. For some reason Merrill hated Jay, and now he saw his way to get rid of an enemy.

And he had an excellent chance of doing just that.

If Jay admitted killing Curtway then he was slated for punishment beneath the Ship's Code. Gregson couldn't cover him up now, not when the accusation had been made public, and even if he could Jay had a shrewd idea that Merrill wouldn't let him. If Jay told the truth, that he hadn't killed Susan's father, then he was in equal danger of elimination from Gregson for having failed his duty. Either way he was in danger of his life and, if George had spoken the truth, Gregson would be merciless. Jay leaned forward as Gregson spoke again.

'You have made an accusation,' he said to Susan. 'Your evidence?'

'I met this man,' again she made a point of not looking at Jay, 'immediately prior to finding the body of my father. There was no reason for him to be in that quarter.'

'Unwarranted assumption,' snapped Gregson. 'That is not proof.'

'I have reason to believe,' she continued

193

stiffly, 'that my father had cause to speak to this man on certain private matters. My father was no duelist and would refuse to fight anyone no matter what the provocation. I suggest that this man was goaded into killing my father because he couldn't murder him in the arena.'

'That isn't true,' blurted Jay. 'I've never fought in the stadium either. I . . . ' He swallowed as he remembered the tell-tale red dot on the inside of his left forearm. As yet he'd had no chance to have it removed and he was acutely conscious of both Merrill and the girl looking at it. 'I did not dislike your father,' he muttered, 'and I didn't want to fight with him.'

'That's not true,' flared Susan. 'My brother will testify that on approaching my father's cubicle, he heard raised voices and this man demanding that my father should meet him in the arena for some fancied insult. Fred, my brother, didn't wish to violate privacy and walked away.' She bit down on her lower lip. 'That was the last time either of us heard my father alive.'

'Still hardly proof of murder,' snapped

Gregson. 'Is that all?'

'Seems pretty conclusive to me,' said Merrill. 'If the brother can swear that West was in the cubicle with Curtway and this girl saw him outside within seconds after finding the body . . . ' He shrugged.

'I did not ask for your opinion,' said Gregson coldly. He looked at Susan. 'Have you any other testimony?'

'When I met him,' Susan gestured towards Jay, 'I noticed something odd about him. We quarreled, never mind about what, and yet he seemed too friendly and wanted to take me away from the area.'

'Perhaps he was sorry for the quarrel and wanted to restore himself in your good graces?'

'No. It wasn't that.' She frowned as if trying to stir her memory. 'There was something else. There was an odor, a horrible burnt kind of smell around him — I don't know how to describe it.' Her face twisted in sudden emotion. 'I smelled the same kind of odor when — '

'The body was burned beyond all

recognition,' explained Merrill to Gregson. 'The charred odor was still very distinctive when I arrived.'

'I see.' Gregson rested his head on the tips of his fingers, his elbows supported on the desk, and stared down at his papers for a moment as if lost in involved thought. Then he looked at the others, his face harsh and bleak, his eyes narrowed as he stared from face to face.

'You have heard the accusation and testimony,' he said to Jay. 'Can you refute them?'

'There is nothing for me to refute,' said Jay easily. 'Surmise, assumption, and sheer coincidence.' He stared appealingly at Susan. 'I did not kill this young lady's father. He was my friend, I knew the entire family, and I swear to her on my hope of life that I did not do as she accuses.'

'Do you believe him?' Gregson stared at Susan.

'You have no real proof,' insisted Gregson. 'Personally, I could hardly bring myself to sentence this man without much firmer evidence. I . . . '

His voice droned on but Jay was hardly listening. He was waiting for the obvious suggestion and, as Gregson spoke, he wondered why it hadn't already been made. There was one certain way to test the guilt or innocence of any man. The lie detectors were part of Psycho, foolproof, almost omnipotent in their efficiency. Susan, as yet, hadn't demanded their use. Perhaps she hadn't thought of it; perhaps, even now, she didn't really believe that he was guilty of the crime, however much outraged feminine pride had made her accuse him. Gregson, of course, wouldn't mention them. As far as he was concerned, Jay had killed the man and any evidence only went to strengthen that belief. The job had been almost criminal in its careless inefficiency, but these things had happened before and, to an extent, were tolerated for one time at least.

Merrill proved to be the Judas.

Susan was wavering, Jay could see that, could see, too, that Gregson would smooth her down, send her on her way and later report the finding of the 'murderer' and his subsequent 'death.' A nice, normal, easy way out of an unpleasant difficulty.

' . . . So you see, my dear,' soothed Gregson, 'you must leave it to us. The psych-police aren't as stupid as some people seem to think. There are certain tests and, even if we have to check every man and woman in the sector, we shall be able to either prove that your father was murdered or that his death was an unfortunate accident.'

'Tests?' Susan frowned. 'How do you mean?'

'The odor you mentioned,' explained Gregson easily. 'We know that tiny particles which constitute what is known as an 'odor' can be found in the skin and clothing of any who were present. There are other things, perspiration index, for one and — '

'The lie detectors,' said Merrill.

'Exactly.' Gregson didn't look at the officer but Jay could tell by the slight writhing of muscle along the edge of the jaw just how Gregson felt. 'As I was saying — '

'This whole thing could be cleared up now,' insisted Merrill. 'Why don't you just put the accused to the test and done with it?' He looked at Susan. 'You'd be satisfied then, wouldn't you? If this man answers truthfully whether or not he killed your father then you could go back and tell the others. If innocent you could clear his name. If guilty . . . ' Merrill shrugged. 'Personally, I'm surprised that he hasn't requested it himself if he's innocent of the charge.'

And that was that.

Numbly Jay grasped the twin electrodes and prepared to answer the questions. There was no hope of evasion, any lie would reveal itself in a flash of red across the signal plate, the truth with a flash of green. In minutes now, seconds even, the truth would come out. He only hoped that part would be revealed, not the whole. He tensed as Gregson leaned forward.

'Did you kill my father?' It was Susan who asked the question. She had risen in her excitement, her eyes anxious as she blurted the question, and Jay could guess

199

that now, after the shock of finding the body had worn off a little, she desperately wanted to find him innocent. Jay looked directly into her eyes as he answered.

Green, a wash of color across the blank surface of the detection plate and, with the glowing color Susan seemed to recover new life.

'I knew it,' she whispered. 'All the time I really knew that you couldn't have done it, but I wasn't sure. Oh, Jay!' She was in his arms then, the wonderful softness of her hair against his cheek and, for a moment, he relaxed to the nearness of her warmth and beauty. Merrill's voice jerked him back to reality.

'It's fixed! The detectors are fixed!' He stared wildly at Gregson, then at Jay. 'you — '

'Be silent!' Gregson rose from his seat and stepped from behind his desk with a smooth coordination of muscular power. 'Take the girl back to her sector and return to duty.'

'You heard my orders, Merrill!'

'I heard them,' said the officer stubbornly, 'but I don't like it.'

'The detectors cannot be 'fixed' as you call it,' snapped Gregson impatiently. 'This man did not kill this girl's father. He is innocent of the accusation.' He stared at Susan. 'You will, of course, spread this information to all who may be interested. You have accused an innocent man and, while I can understand and sympathize with your emotional upset, you still owe it both to the psych-police and to Jay West to undo the harm you may have done.' He pointed towards the door. 'You may leave now. Merrill! Obey your orders.'

For a moment the officer hesitated, doubt struggling with his own knowledge; then, as he stared at Gregson's taut features, he shrugged and led the way from the inner office. Jay was about to follow him when Gregson called him back.

'Not you, West. Stay here.'

Jay knew what was coming. Had known it from the first. He had not killed the man he should; Gregson knew it, Merrill would have, too, if he had stopped to think on the exact phraseology of the question, and now he had to answer for his failure. Tiredly he slumped back into the chair.

'You were lucky,' said Gregson unexpectedly. 'Did you realize that?'

Jay shrugged, not answering.

'If the question had been 'Did you kill a man?' your answer would have automatically convicted you to death by torture. Psycho would have seen to that, or the Captain rather, which is much the same thing.' Gregson stared thoughtfully at the young man. 'Who did you kill?'

'Curtway.'

'Don't bother to lie to me, West. Merrill may think that the detectors have been fixed, but I know that they haven't. You didn't kill George Curtway. You killed someone else and planted the body in the place of your assignment.' Gregson nodded. 'I'd wondered about your apparent carelessness; sloppy work isn't like you, and that job was ludicrously inefficient on the surface. You had to choose electrocution because nothing else would have disfigured the body beyond recognition.'

Gregson nodded again as if pleased at solving a problem. 'Who was it?'

'Sam Aldway.' Jay pointed to the assignment card on the desk. 'I'm anticipating. You can cross him off already.'

'And Curtway?'

Jay remained silent.

'You've failed in your duty, West,' said Gregson coldly, and now there was no trace of his former friendliness in his tone. 'You know the penalty for that.' He leaned forward and stared at Jay. 'Why did you let him live?'

Gregson didn't use the lie detectors, the obvious and simplest method of acquiring tested information and, looking at the chief of psych-police, Jay began to guess why. Tests on the detectors were recorded on tape and transmitted to Psycho. Others could possibly replay that information, the Captain certainly, though there was no indication that he ever did. Gregson was being cautious and, realizing that fact, Jay felt a first glimmer of hope.

'I'm in love with his daughter,' he

admitted. 'I just couldn't eliminate her father.'

'It that your only reason?'

'Yes. Sam Aldway, the man I killed, picked a quarrel with me.' Jay shrugged. 'I saw a chance to make the switch and took it.'

'I see.' Gregson sighed with something like relief. 'You know that Psycho determined Curtway's death and you know that it is our job to eliminate the unfit as ordered by the machine?'

'I do.'

'You know too the penalty for inefficiency?'

'Yes.'

'You're in trouble, West,' said Gregson softly. 'If I relay this information to Psycho, Merrill will take great pleasure in eliminating you.' He paused. 'Where is Curtway?'

'I don't know.'

'But you could find him?'

'Yes, I think so.'

'Find him, West,' ordered Gregson. 'Find him and eliminate him. When you have done that notify me personally so that I can examine the body. Do that and I'll forget to relay your inefficiency to Psycho.' He smiled without humor and, watching him, Jay was reminded more than ever of a feline.

'Find and kill that man, West — or *die*.'

He was still smiling as Jay left the office.

13

The ship was a murmuring throb of whispering sound. The eternal, inevitable vibration of life trapped in a medium of emptiness and silence. It was comforting in a way to hear it, to feel the subtle quiver of footsteps, the soft drone of engines, the myriad sounds of five thousand people living and breathing, loving and hoping, playing and working in the titanic metal egg which was their universe and their home. George Curtway had known that sound all his life, had been born to it, lived with it, felt it as a part of him. Now, lying in the thick, almost tangible darkness of No-Weight, he clung to it as the one familiar thing in a world of terror.

He was afraid.

He was afraid of the darkness, the emptiness, the unseen vastness of the space around the central axis. Never before in his life had he been in any space larger than the exercise rooms; there had always been others around him, and even in the privacy of his own cubicle or the common tee-rooms, he'd had the comforting knowledge that others were within a few yards of him. Now, suffering from the twin fears of darkness and agoraphobia, he stared, wide eyed into the surrounding darkness.

He had not moved far since Jay had left him. He had tried to sleep a little, but had not felt tired. He didn't feel hungry either, and had long ago lost all track of time.

He could have drifted in darkness for an hour, or a week, or a month. He didn't know.

He started as a slight sound came from the darkness before him, a soft, almost inaudible scraping, a sound as of an indrawn breath, the slight stir of disturbed air. It wasn't the first time he had heard such sounds but he didn't yield to superstitious terrors. Ghosts, goblins, elves, fairies, ghouls and vampires, the whole realm and terminology of the shadow-world of darkness and night, had died for the Ship's personnel when they had left their own world. If there was a noise in the darkness, then it must have been made by living persons, and George wanted to know who they were.

'Who's there?'

Silence. The smothered sound of a laugh. Again the scraping as of someone kicking against metal and launching himself through space. Cautiously George shifted his position and strained his ears for further betraying sounds.

The clang of metal ruined his concentration, and light, streaming through an open hatch, caught his attention. A dark shape squeezed through the opening as George kicked himself towards it.

'Jay?'

'Is that you, George?' The young officer drew himself clear of the hatch, reached out and swung the door shut after him. 'Let's get away from here.'

'What's happened?' George allowed himself to be led away from the hatch, gripping the arm of the officer tightly as they drifted through darkness towards an unknown destination.

'Gregson knows that you're still alive.' Rapidly Jay told of the accusation, impromptu trial, and Gregson's ultimatum. 'He followed me, of course, but I had expected that. I managed to dodge him long enough for me to pass through the hatch.' Jay swore as metal bruised his face. 'Waste! Why can't we have lights in here?'

Light came at that moment, a shaft of brilliance from the newly opened hatch, and a man's head and shoulders were visible as he peered into No-Weight. Jay twisted as he stared towards the illumination and caught a dimly-seen girder to steady himself.

'Gregson. If he finds us he'll kill us both.'

'If he can,' said George grimly. He stared at the barely revealed latticework of stanchions and girders. 'Even with lights he'll have a hard job to find us in here.'

'He knows that.' Jay grunted as the hatch slammed shut and darkness returned. 'He'll lock the door and seal us in. Let's hope that he'll be satisfied to leave us alone now.'

'You think he will?' George didn't sound too hopeful. As the darkness closed around them, he felt a return of his unfamiliar fears and, even though now he had company, he didn't relish the thought of spending an indefinite period in the loneliness of No-Weight.

'No,' admitted Jay. 'He wants us dead. You because for some reason he's afraid of you, and me because I let you live.' In the darkness he sought and found the other's arm. 'What's all this about, George? Why should Gregson be afraid of you?'

'I told you, Jay. I found out that he has cheated on Psycho and avoided his own death.'

'So you told me, but what proof have you? Even if you did manage to get to the Captain and make your accusation, could you make it stick?' Jay wiped at his forehead, half-annoyed with himself to find it moist with perspiration. Now that the swift rush of action was over, he felt the emotional collapse of the reaction and its attendant depression.

Like it or not, he was as good as dead.

Trapped in No-Weight he would starve or die of thirst. The exits were all guarded, the emergency hatches locked and, even if Gregson left them alone, neither he nor George had any chance of reaching the Captain. In effect, they had chosen to hide in their own tomb.

'Once we get to the Captain,' George said. 'I can prove what I say.' He hesitated. 'Do you know anything about electronics, Jay? Or the workings of Psycho?'

'A little, not much.'

'Psycho is a kind of electronic sieve. Everyone has a card — it's really a sheet of metallic plastic impressed with varying degrees of magnetism — and those cards are sorted and compared to a master plate in the machine itself. All cards not meeting specifications are ejected. You know what happens to them better than I do, but that isn't important. I only guessed at the real purpose of those cards after I had made my check and found out what had happened.'

'And that was?'

'That totals of the cards issued, the

cards remaining, and the cards erased should always be the same. In other words the Ship left Earth with a certain amount of cards. That total should now be the same. Well, it isn't.'

'Perhaps they lost one,' said Jay. 'Or destroyed one.'

'No. Those cards operate on a closed circuit. They are ejected, erased, re-filed and re-used. A record is kept of the exact number at each stage of the operation together with a punched tape signifying disposals, etc.' George paused. 'I found that there are two cards missing.'

'That isn't important,' Jay snapped irritably. 'I've seen those cards. Perhaps someone lost one in some way. Waste, George! In three hundred years it wouldn't be hard to lose a card or two.'

'You miss the point, Jay.' George sounded as if he were explaining why two and two should always make four. 'The cards you've seen aren't the ones from the machines. When I talk of ejected cards I don't mean the copies you've seen. The cards themselves remain within Psycho. Once scanned and found wanting, a copy of name and number is made, the copy ejected and the original erased and re-filed. The copies are usable more than once. In effect no card, as I use the term, ever leaves the machine.'

'So? Where does that get us?'

'Someone has tampered with Psycho. Has located two cards, removed them, and possibly destroyed them.' George sighed at the other's silence. 'Can't you see it yet, Jay? Suppose that your card is in the machine. You know that one day, you don't know just when, that card will be scanned and ejected. When that happens, you know that you are due to die. You don't want to die. What do you do?'

'Take out the card,' Jay answered automatically, then swore. 'Is that what happened? Is it possible?'

'Yes, to both questions. It is possible, if you know all about the machine. I might be able to do it — but it wouldn't be easy.'

'Gregson?'

'He would have to be in on it. As chief of psych-police he would be the first to get curious and suspicious.'

'But he couldn't remove the cards?'

'Who then?'

'I don't know,' said George slowly. 'I've not had time to give this thing much thought. I only stumbled upon the discrepancy in the grand totals a short while ago, and you know what's happened since then. I knew that Gregson must be implicated because of his position but even then I didn't know about the program of elimination. You taught me about that, though I had had my suspicions as I told you.'

'It doesn't make sense,' protested Jay. 'Why should Gregson do that? All he needed to have done was to wait until his card was ejected and then destroy it. As chief of psych-police no one need ever have known.'

'It couldn't have been as simple as that, Jay. Other men have been in Gregson's position, and I assume that they were all eliminated when their turn came.' George sucked in his breath. 'You know, the more I think about it the more complicated it all becomes.

Who eliminates the psych-police? Who decides when the chief is due for death? There must be some check or safeguard, Jay — if there weren't we'd have had a despotism centuries ago.'

'We know our responsibilities,' Jay said curtly. He didn't want to explain how each officer carried the knowledge of his fate with him . . . how, sometimes in the silent darkness of their lonely cubicles, they awoke to sweating fear of the unavoidable. He blinked in a sudden flood of light.

'The lights!' George stared at the rows of glowing tubes. 'Someone's turned on the lights!'

'Gregson.' Jay felt a sudden nausea as he looked at the immensity of No-Weight and clutched at a girder for support. He had never, in all his life, seen anything as big before. It was incredible in its sheer vastness, a colossal tube fully a hundred yards across, so long that its sides diminished in perspective. Girders ringed a complex latticework of thick metal struts and stanchions, webbed in the center to a unified hole from which spread the ranked layers of the Ship itself.

'It's big,' whispered George and his knuckles as he gripped the stanchion showed white beneath the strain. 'It must be the biggest thing in the Ship.'

Which, of course, wasn't true. No-Weight, because of the preponderance of girders and essential fabric, the low gravity at the perimeter and the absence of it at the central axis, was merely the largest unused space in the Ship. Even at that the builders had found a use for it. Stale air, rising from the lower levels, was piped to No-Weight where it was in turn blown down to the gardens, there to be circulated over the acres of carbondioxide removing plants and adjusted for optimum human consumption. But to a man whose horizon had always been the metal walls of cubicle or corridor, No-Weight was big.

Sounds echoed through the silence; the clang of metal and the soft shuffle of distant feet. Down the brilliantly lit tube, looking tiny and insignificant against the incredible thickness of the girders, men streamed through an open door. Jay looked at them, narrowing his eyes as he tried to focus on the unaccustomed distance, then turned his head as similar sounds echoed from near at hand.

'What's happening?' whispered George, instinctively keeping his voice low in the echoing vastness. 'Who are they? What are they doing here?'

'Gregson,' said Jay again, and tasted a bitterness in his mouth as he looked at the new arrivals. They were strangers but he recognized the type. The hangers on at the stadiums, the men who found pleasure in watching pain and struggle, the frustrated beings who, denied the very thing for which they had been bred, found escape in personal combat and vicarious battle. Others were among them, familiar shapes wearing the black shorts of the psych-police and, from the hands of both police and strangers, little flashes of metallic brilliance sparkled and died, flared again and dulled, flashing as the bright lights reflected from the polished surfaces.

'Knives,' said George wonderingly. 'They're carrying knives.'

'They're going to search No-Weight,'

explained Jay. 'They've entered by two doors and will search the sector between. When that's done they'll move along until we'll be trapped against one of the ends.' He squinted down the length of the tube. 'See? They've started towards the engines and will sweep towards the sealed areas.'

'Can we escape?' George looked hopefully at the officer. 'What about that hatch by which you entered?'

'Gregson would have locked it after him.' Jay shook his head. 'We can hide, I suppose — it's going to take them a long time to sweep through the central axis, but they'll get us in the end.' He stared at the knives in the hands of the searchers. 'Gregson must be desperate to do a thing like this.'

He fell silent, crouching behind a girder and watching the skilled maneuvering of the searchers. Their plan was simple and, because of that, was highly effective. A party moved out to the central girders and, at a signal, moved forward and around it. Nothing living or dead could escape being seen by them. A second party waited a little behind the first, resting poised and ready, their knives in their hands and prepared to dart after and attack anyone who eluded the searchers. The two parties moved forward together while a third group, smaller than the others, strung themselves along the examined area.

'Can we dodge past them?' George ducked behind the girder and looked appealingly at Jay. 'They'll hardly search the entire area twice.'

'They'll search until we're found and killed,' said Jay grimly. He kept his voice low knowing how sound traveled in the silence of No-Weight, knowing too that it was only because the searchers were concentrating on their immediate vicinity and not worrying about what lay ahead, that they had not been seen when the lights went on. He kept the bulk of the girder between them and the searchers as he spoke to George.

'Gregson's thought of everything.' He jerked his head towards the searchers. 'They're even wearing white arm bands. That's to stop us mingling with them and pretending that we belong to the party.

They would hardly know us by sight and, as far as Gregson knows, we could have knives of our own.'

'What can we do? Have you any ideas, Jay?'

'Not yet,' Jay glared at the lights. 'If it weren't for those we could sneak past and maybe break out into the Ship. We could even attack a couple of the searchers and take their arm bands and knives.' He glanced at the electronics engineer. 'Can't you kill the lights in some way?'

'Not from in here. The wires and fuses are all in the outer corridors, and even if we managed to smash the protective cover and short a tube, it wouldn't extinguish the others.' He stepped towards one of the lights. 'You want me to do that?'

'No. If you killed only one it would just attract attention.' Jay peered around the edge of the girder and jerked back his head as he saw how near the searchers were. 'Come on, George,' he whispered. 'We've got to get moving. Follow me, stay close to the wall, and always keep a girder between you and the advance party. Ready?'

Gravity was so low that they could literally skim over the 'floor.' Jay led the way, thrusting himself along with calculated force, judging things so that he could cushion his impact with his hands and arms. Rapidly, they passed along the central axis towards the sealed areas, not stopping until the searchers were far behind. Then they paused for breath.

'Can we escape, Jay?'

'I don't think so.' Jay stared around at the silent girders. 'This part of the Ship is strange to me, but Gregson must know the locale well enough to know that we can't get out.'

'I see.' George sat thinking for a moment, then he looked at the younger man. 'Look. I got you into this, Jay, and maybe I can get you out. Suppose you took me prisoner and delivered me to Gregson? That would save your life, wouldn't it? And later, after it was all over, you could tell the Captain what I told you about the tampering with Psycho.'

'No.'

'Be reasonable, Jay. What's the good of

both of us getting killed if one can escape? I don't think that I'd mind dying so much if I knew that Gregson would be taken care of afterwards. I'm an old man, Jay, and I don't suppose that I could live much longer, but you're young.' He hesitated. 'There's another thing. I'd like to feel that there was someone to look after Susan. You know what I mean.'

'Look, George,' Jay explained patiently, 'it wouldn't work. Gregson can't afford to let me live now, and once he reports my inefficiency to Psycho, I'll be due for elimination. He may already have done so. In any case, those searchers probably have orders to kill every living thing they find. We'd never get past the first group, let alone down into the Ship itself.' He shook his head, then tensed as he heard a sound. 'What was that?'

'I don't know,' whispered George. 'It sounded like a laugh or — ' He broke off as the sound was repeated. 'Could they have reached us already?'

'I doubt it.' Jay listened again, then stared towards a girder. 'Stay here.'

He moved carefully to avoid the

slightest possibility of noise, and stepped lightly towards the girder from behind which the sound had come. He reached it, peered around it — and stared.

The man who cowered behind the girder was naked, his pallid skin grimed with dirt so that it looked almost gray in the brilliant lighting. He tittered as he saw Jay, his deeplined face convulsed with horrible merriment, and his eyes peered through a tangled mat of waist-length hair. It was that hair which made Jay doubt whether the creature was really human. He stared at it, hardly believing his eyes, looking from the hair to the bloated limbs, the filthy skin, the scabrous, unhealthy looking flesh.

'What is it?' George gripped Jay's arm as he stared at the monstrosity. 'Is it a man?'

'Yes.'

'But look at it! That hair!'

'It's white,' Jay whispered slowly. 'White hair! Is it possible for a man to have white hair?'

All the Ship personnel had brown or black hair with a little red and some blond. White hair was a sign of age and no ordinary member of the Ship's personnel had ever seen an old man. He recoiled a little as the stranger lunged to his feet.

'Food,' he mouthed. 'Food.'

'He's insane,' stated Jay decisively. 'No sane man would let himself get into such a state of filth.' He stepped back as the man advanced towards them, his hands held before him, a thin trickle of saliva running from the corner of his mouth. 'Food,' he whined. 'Don't forget poor old Joe. Joe's hungry. They didn't leave him anything to eat.'

'Who didn't?' Jay forced himself to grip the man by the shoulder. 'Which others?'

'The rest.' The stranger gestured vaguely around him. 'We lived here, all alone in the dark.' He tittered again. 'I like the dark. I like to float in the emptiness and drift from place to place.' His face crinkled as if he were going to cry. 'But I'm hungry. Poor old Joe, no one wants him now. No one at all.'

Looking at him, Jay could believe that. The man could arouse nothing but abhorrence in any who saw him. He gritted his teeth as he shook the obese figure.

'Who are you? How did, you get here?'

'I'm Joe,' whined the creature. 'They wanted to kill me so I ran away.' He giggled. 'I fooled them. They couldn't kill old Joe. Joe was too clever for them, Joe was.' He giggled again and held out his hands. 'Food?'

'That must have been what I heard while I was waiting for you,' said George. He told Jay of the sounds which had troubled him while resting in the darkness. 'Is it possible that others have run away to hide in No-Weight?'

'I don't know,' said Jay slowly. He frowned, remembering vague rumors of people who had escaped their fate by flight to what he had always thought was a living tomb.

'How long have you lived here?' George asked.

'A long time,' tittered the man. He seemed pleased to have an audience. 'A long, long time. Others came after me, but I've lived the longest.'

'Which others?' Jay questioned. 'Where are they?'

'They ran away when the lights came on,' complained the man. 'I don't like the lights, they hurt my eyes, but they didn't care about that. They just left me, all of them, and they didn't leave me any food.' He held out his hands again in an oddly disturbing gesture. 'Food? You'll feed poor old Joe?'

'Later.' Jay stared at George. 'There must have been others hiding in No-Weight besides this wreck. Somehow they obtained food and managed to live.' He nodded thoughtfully as he thought about it. 'Food requirements would be low in the absence of gravity and lack of physical exercise would account for his fat. Lack of water would account for his dirt, though he could probably lick enough condensation from the metal to stay alive.'

'What about his hair?' asked George. He shuddered as he looked at the tangled mass. 'Look at it! It's disgusting!'

'Never mind his hair.' Jay stared at the man again, trying to ignore his odor, his dirt, the saliva drooling from his mouth and the restless twitching of his eyes. 'Joe!'

'You want me? You want old Joe?'

'Those others you spoke of — where are they?'

'They ran away.' A cunning expression crept over the lined face. 'You want to find them?'

'Yes.'

'They've got food. You'll fetch it back to poor old Joe?'

'Yes.' Jay glanced down the tube towards the nearing searchers. 'If you'll tell me where to find them, I'll get some food for you. Where are they?'

'Down there.' The man gestured towards the sealed areas. 'They ran away when the lights came on. Bosco, and Murray and the rest. They all ran away from me.' Tears of self-pity glistened in the restless eyes. 'Food?'

'Where did they go?'

'I told you.' Again the man gestured towards the end of the central axis. 'Somewhere down there. They know where the food is but they wouldn't tell me.' He sniffed, wiping his nose on the back of his hand, a gesture which almost caused Jay to vomit. George pulled at his arm, his face anxious.

'Hurry, Jay,' he whispered. 'We'll be seen soon.'

'Coming.' Jay stared hopelessly at the lined features of the stranger, knowing that he had obtained all the information he could from the creature, and yet knowing that it wasn't enough. For a moment he hesitated, then, as the first of the searchers came into view, he followed George towards the end of the tube.

They had passed two sets of girders when they heard the shout and for a second Jay thought that they had been seen. Then the shouts turned into laughter, against a background of screams. Jay stared grimly at the electronics engineer.

'Still want to give yourself up?'

'They killed him,' George said sickly. 'An old man like that, and they killed him.'

Jay didn't answer, but progressed with increased speed towards the blank metal ahead. A riveted bulkhead sealed off No-Weight from the mysterious regions of the sealed areas beyond and Jay stared at it, biting his lips as he looked for signs of the 'others' whom the insane creature had mentioned. George gripped his arm.

'Look! A door! See?'

A small hatchway was open at the edge of the bulkhead. It was a round panel, three feet across and opening inwards so that it looked like a dark spot against the polished smoothness of the bulkhead. From where they stood it was 'up' and a little to the right, almost directly opposite across a hundred yards of clear space. Even as they looked at it, the panel began to close.

Jay gripped a strut, twisted himself so that his feet rested against the metal and, aiming quickly, thrust himself with the full power of his muscles towards the closing door. It was a risky thing he did. His speed was too great for safety and, as he hurtled across the clear space, he knew that he would land too heavily. He twisted his body as he passed the central region where gravity abruptly altered so that, instead of the hatchway being 'up,' it now became 'down,' and plummeted feet-first towards the panel.

He hit with a force which jarred the teeth in his head and sent little shafts of pain lancing up his legs and thighs. For a moment he was afraid that the door had been locked and that he had broken his bones against the unyielding surface. Then the panel gave beneath him, he hurtled through the hatchway and he was in darkness, struggling with something soft and yielding. A man swore, then hands closed around his throat and a voice rasped terse instructions.

'Shut that door! Quick!'

'Here's another.' A man, a shapeless figure against the light, grunted as George gripped the edge of the hatchway.

'Get him inside,' snapped the first voice. 'Quick!'

Light flared with the closing of the hatch and, in the dim glow of a hand-beam, Jay blinked up at the first speaker. He was a big man, stocky, with mottled gray hair. He stared at Jay, saw the black uniform shorts, and his hands tightened with grim promise.

'Police!'

'No.' Jay tore at the hands around his throat, gripping the fingers and wrenching them free. 'Bosco? Murray?'

'How did you know my name?' The big man rubbed his injured hands and glared at Jay. 'I'm Bosco.'

'Joe told me.' Jay looked towards where George was held by the other man. 'We're on the run from Gregson, the chief of psych-police. Those searchers are after us. They killed the old man, Joe he said his name was, and they'll kill us too if they find us.'

'Why?'

'I escaped into No-Weight,' said George quickly. 'Jay here helped me.'

'You came to join the Barbs?' Bosco glared suspiciously at Jay. 'You? An officer?'

'I had no choice,' Jay explained grimly. 'I should have killed George, eliminated him, but I didn't. Gregson found out and now he wants us both dead.' Jay stared curiously at Bosco. 'Are you Barbs?'

'Yes. We're the barbarians, so called because we wanted to live.' There was a brittle dryness in the big man's voice. 'We skulk in No-Weight, eating when we can, drinking what we can, living how we can. You should know of us.'

'I've heard rumors,' admitted Jay, 'but that's all. I'd begun to doubt if you really existed.'

'A policy of silence,' Bosco nodded. 'It makes sense — the less who know of us the fewer there will be wanting to join us.' He looked at his companion. 'What shall we do with these two?'

'Throw them back into No-Weight.' The man who held George glowered at his captive. 'If it hadn't been for these two the police might never have wanted to search. We only just got away in time as it is.'

'We can't throw them back,' snapped Bosco. 'If we leave them alive, they'll talk, and if we kill them first someone will begin asking questions. Waste!' He glared at Jay. 'Why did you have to follow us?'

'I wanted to live,' said Jay quietly. He looked at the gray-haired man. 'Like you, like Murray here, like Joe.'

'Joe was too far gone to save.' Bosco didn't seem to like talking about it. 'The searchers expect to find some Barbs living in No-Weight, and we had to leave some for them to find. Joe, Mary, Sam, a few others. All of them old-timers. Joe had lived here for over thirty years and was insane for the past ten. The darkness finally got him — that and other things.' He didn't explain what those 'other things' might have been. 'It's best that they should die to save the rest. They were due for the converters years ago.' He looked at Murray again. 'Well?'

Murray shrugged. He had made his suggestion and didn't seem able or willing to make others. George spoke before the big man could make up his mind.

'Can't we wait here until the search is over? We'll promise not to tell anyone about what we've seen.'

'How can we trust him?' Murray jerked his thumb towards Jay. 'A policeman. Waste! He'll have the Ship aroused as soon as he got to a phone.'

'The Ship will be aroused anyway,' said Jay easily. 'You forget, Gregson is looking for us, not you. When he doesn't find us he's going to start wondering. As far as anyone knows at the moment there is no way out of No-Weight except the guarded entries. As soon as his men report that we aren't in here, Gregson will order an investigation. He may even go to the Captain.'

'The Captain?' Bosco glanced at Murray, an odd expression in his eyes. 'Why should he do that?'

'Because he knows that's where we are trying to go.' Jay smiled at the big man. 'George here has something to tell him, something Gregson will do anything to prevent the Captain from hearing. If he misses us now, and he will, then he'll become desperate. On the other hand, if you take us to the Captain, or help us get to him, then maybe I can put in a good word for you.'

'What could you do for us?' Murray released George and stepped forward, his face coming into greater clarification as he neared the source of light. Like Bosco his hair was shot with gray and his features wore an unusual hardness. Jay shrugged.

'I don't know yet. An amnesty,

perhaps? Something like that. But it all depends on the Captain.'

'Yes.' Murray seemed to be secretly amused. 'It does, doesn't it.' He glanced at Bosco. 'Think we should do it?'

'Why not? We can't throw them back into No-Weight and I don't fancy killing them here. They could be telling the truth, or they might be lying to save their own skins. It doesn't matter. If they're trying to be clever, we can eliminate them later.' He jerked his head towards Jay and George. 'Come on with us, then. Stay close behind and don't try anything.' He was turning away when Jay caught at his arm.

'Where are you taking us?'

'To join the rest of us who escaped that trap.' Bosco led the way from the cubicle into a wide corridor.

It was bitterly cold, so cold that Jay felt his skin goose pimple and his teeth chatter. Next to him George moaned with discomfort and rubbed his arms to try and keep them warm. The two Barbs, aside from their pluming breath, didn't appear to react to the chill, and Jay guessed that to them it was no new experience.

A light winked ahead of them; Bosco answered the signal and, within seconds, they had come up with the rest of the party. Jay stared with interest at them. There were eight men and four women, and all had the same indefinable stamp of something outside his experience. The hair of some, like that of Bosco and Murray, was shot with silver threads, but it wasn't that which made them seem almost alien to the officer. It was something about their eyes, the unconscious attitude of superiority and self-mastery so that, beside them, he felt as he were a child. They stared at him, listening to Bosco's explanation, then together the assembled party continued down the icy corridor.

It grew colder as they went on but the gravity remained the same and Jay knew that they were progressing along one of the communicating tubes running beside No-Weight. They had walked a long way and Jay was numb and George blue with the cold when Bosco halted before a door.

'Don't touch anything you may see out there.' He gestured to beyond the panel. 'The rest know about it, but you're new. Remember, don't touch anything.'

He snapped off his hand beam as he swung open the panel and Jay blinked to a flood of light.

It came from one end of a vast chamber in a wave of brilliance almost too great for eyes accustomed to the dimness of the corridor, but, as Jay blinked and stared, he could see a multitude of brilliant points against a background darker than the shorts he wore.

'They're moving!' whispered George, and his voice echoed his amazement. 'Those lights are moving!'

They were. They moved from one side of the blackness down in a smooth arc to disappear at the other, while new ones took their place as they passed in continual procession across the darkness. To George it was the strangest lighting system he had ever seen and to Jay it was inexplicable. He turned and touched Bosco's arm.

'What is it?'

'That?' Bosco looked towards the glittering points. 'Oh, they're stars.'

'Stars!'

'That's right. You've heard of stars, haven't you?' Jay had, but only as a repeated lecture on one of the tapes; to him the word 'star' had nothing to do with reality, and he stared at the scene in bewildered amazement.

'Come on,' Bosco said urgently. 'We mustn't linger here. The very temperature of our bodies can affect the instruments.' He began to drag Jay towards the far wall of the vast room. 'Let's get moving before we freeze.'

Reluctantly Jay turned and followed Bosco, his head riding on his shoulder as he stared back at the glittering display of the universe. Suddenly he tripped and almost fell over a vat-like receptacle. It was one of many ranked in orderly rows across the floor, and as Jay caught at the edge to save himself from falling, he stared directly into the face of a dead man.

He rested beneath a sheet of some transparent material, still, immobile, the lips parted a trifle to reveal glistening teeth, the eyes closed and the body — a surprisingly undeveloped body, according to Jay's standards — naked and with a waxen pallid look.

Jay had heard of deep freeze, all the Ship personnel had, but to him deep freeze was where the animals and birds, the fish and insectivores lay against the time of their awakening at Journey's End. No one had ever dreamed that men too could lie in suspended animation. No one, that is, of the ordinary Ship personnel, and Jay's immediate assumption was that they must be dead.

He couldn't guess that here in these ranked vats rested the brains, technology and filtered information of a world three hundred years away in time and uncountable miles in space. Here were the ecologists, the atomic engineers, the rocket pilots, the geologists, the mineralogists, and the specialists in all the other branches of science and experience impossible to either teach or practice in the Ship itself. They rested as they had rested ever since the Ship had left Earth, sleeping, if it could be called that, waiting for the day when they would be wakened to help build a new Earth.

But to Jay they were all dead men.

As he stared at Bosco waiting impatiently for him at the far side of the chamber, his eyes were dull with lack of understanding.

'What kept you so long?'

'Those men,' stammered Jay. 'I saw them.'

'Well?'

'They're dead. All dead.'

'What of it?' Bosco stared at Jay as he led the way into a corridor. 'Haven't you ever seen a dead man before?'

'Yes, but . . . ' Jay swallowed, hardly noticing that it grew warmer as they walked down the passageway. 'Why weren't they sent to the converters? Why keep them like that?'

'I don't know,' Bosco said thoughtfully. 'I've wondered about that myself. As far as I know there is only one man who could answer that.'

'Who?'

'The man we are going to see. The Captain.'

Jay was so numbed with repeated shocks that he didn't even feel surprised.

14

The scene was a normal one of distant Earth, a farming scene with animals and crops, machines and happy, busy men and women. Malick smiled as he saw it, leaning a little forward as he stared at the illuminated screen of the viewer. The children would be seeing the same educational tape; remembrance of their planet of origin was an essential part of Ship indoctrination.

The scene changed as he watched, the harvesters climbing into an animal-drawn vehicle, and the images moved to portray their faces in enlarged close-ups. The women were young, healthy, radiant with fitness and enjoyment; the men, also young, also fit, comfortably attired in loose shirts and trousers. The driver —

Malick felt almost physically ill.

It was the shock of the unexpected which did it. The man was normal enough, with two arms, two legs, two eyes and a head, but there was something about him which the geneticist had never seen before.

White hair. Lined features. Gnarled hands.

The man was old.

The screen faded as Malick turned the switch and picked up his phone. 'Gregson?'

'Speaking.'

'Malick here. I've just seen a new tape. One relayed to the children.'

'So?'

'So it shows an old man. Do you understand, Gregson? An old man!'

'How do you know?' There was irritated impatience in the chief's voice. 'Have you ever seen an old man?'

'Of course I have. Quentin is old, isn't he? Well, so was the man I saw in pictures on the tape.' Malick gripped the phone with sudden urgency. 'Gregson! Don't you realize what this could mean?'

'Yes,' said Gregson after a pause. 'Yes, I see what you're getting at.'

'It could ruin our social system,' babbled Malick. 'Once the children get used to the idea that a man is only old when he has white hair, lined features and gnarled hands, then who's going to believe that they're old at forty?'

'You don't have to explain to me what I already know, said Gregson coldly. 'Is this the first time you've seen the tape?'

'Yes. I'd noticed something odd before — you remember, the tapes showing people slaughtering animals and eating meat. You laughed at me then, but this time you can't afford to laugh. What do you think will happen when the children grow up and begin asking questions?'

'Trouble,' snapped Gregson curtly. 'Look. Have you any witnesses to what you saw?'

'No. But I can find some. It's a certainty that one or more of the attendants would have watched the tapes. I'll find someone if you like.'

'Do that. Find her and fetch her up to the Bridge.'

'The Bridge?'

'That's right.' Gregson sounded unnaturally grim. 'This is a matter which has to be settled by the Captain.'

'But . . .'

The voice died as Gregson replaced his handset. Merrill, lounging on the edge of the desk, looked curiously at his superior officer. 'What was that all about?'

'My business.' Gregson glared impatiently at the young man. 'What are you doing here, anyway? I ordered every officer into No-Weight to conduct the search.'

'The search is finished,' said Merrill easily. 'I've taken back the dueling knives you issued out to the men, and returned them to the stadiums. The men themselves have gone back to their work.'

'Did you find them?'

'Who?'

'You know who I mean, Merrill. West and Curtway. Did you find them?'

'We found and eliminated seven people. Five women and two men.' Merrill paused with calculated deliberation. 'Jay and his friend were not among them.'

'What?'

'We didn't find either of the two men you wanted.'

'That's impossible! I watched Jay enter

No-Weight and I know that Curtway was hiding there. Waste, Merrill! Are you telling me that you've fallen down on the job?'

'I'm telling you that we couldn't find people who weren't there to be found.'

'Impossible!'

'Keep saying that,' Merrill sneered. 'I tell you that we searched No-Weight from one end to the other and we eliminated everyone we found. Jay and Curtway weren't to be found, therefore they couldn't have been in No-Weight.' Merrill slipped from the edge of the desk and stared down at his chief. 'To me that's simple logic — unless you want me to believe that they were invisible and slipped through solid metal.'

'I can't understand it.' Gregson stared suspiciously at the young officer, his hatred and fear returning with renewed force. Merrill was getting to be dangerous. The man was ambitious, too ambitious, and, now that Jay had let him down, Gregson knew that he would have to find a new weapon against Merrill, and fast. He gestured towards the door.

'Return to duty.'

Merrill hesitated, wondering whether now wouldn't be the best time to eliminate his chief and so gain his coveted position. He could do it so easily; next to him, Gregson was an old man and long out of practice in the delicate art of killing a man with his bare hands. Memory of Quentin and his warning came just as he was about to reach for the other's throat. Sucking in his breath, Merrill forced himself to control his emotions. He turned just as he reached the door.

'When are you going to see the Captain?'

'Why?'

'I thought that perhaps you'd like me to come with you.' Merrill smiled with superior knowledge. 'After all, as I conducted the search the Captain might like to have a first-hand report on what we found.'

'I'll relay the report,' snapped Gregson. He stared pointedly at the young man. 'Return to your duty and leave the thinking to me.'

'Yes, *sir!*' Merrill made the title sound like an insult.

Gregson sighed as he stared at the closing door and, despite his iron calm, felt a mounting sense of danger. Jay and Curtway had escaped the search, a search for which he alone was responsible. The Barbs were dead, yes, but the death of seven people would hardly justify arming Ship personnel, taking them from their normal duties, and the power-loss caused by illuminating the entire area of No-Weight.

And Jay and Curtway were still alive.

Jay didn't matter; that is, he hadn't mattered until now, but if Curtway had told him what he knew, and if Merrill had found them, listened to them and hidden them somewhere, waiting for his chance to take them to the Captain . . .

Gregson stared down at the surface of his desk and his face grew bleak as he visualized what must be the outcome of any such move. He shivered a little as if at a return of his recurrent dream, feeling in imagination the plastic bag of the men in olive, the sharp knives of the medical

248

students, the final violation of the dreaded converters. All of that would happen if they reached the Captain. But if he were the Captain . . .

Gregson reached for the phone, punched a number, and waited impatiently for the connection to be made.

'Yes?'

'Gregson here. Conway?'

'That's right.' Anxiety sharpened the psychologist's voice. 'Anything wrong?'

'Plenty. Too many people know too much. Curtway for one.'

'But you told me that he was dead.'

'I thought that he was, but he isn't. Never mind that now.' Gregson glanced towards the door and lowered his voice. 'Listen. Psycho must eject the cards of Jay West — got that?'

'Jay West, yes?'

'And Merrill. Both psych-police officers. You have their numbers on file. I want those men slated for elimination and the sooner you have their cards ejected the better. Can you do it now?'

'Now?' Conway sounded troubled. 'I don't know. It won't be as simple as last time. You want me to locate those cards, alter them or the master plate so that they will fail to meet specifications, and return the machine to normal.'

'Feed in the following data,' snapped Gregson. 'Both are guilty of inefficiency in that both have aroused suspicion through sloppy work. Merrill has delusions of grandeur, Jay is paranoid. Waste, Conway! This is *important!* Can you do it or can't you?'

'I'll try.' Conway didn't sound too hopeful. 'Why, Gregson, is something wrong?'

'Yes.' Gregson paused, letting the tension of the psychologist mount, then spoke again with sharp urgency. 'Curtway knows what we've done. Jay West knows it too, and I think that Merrill has a suspicion. All of them want to reach the Captain.' He paused again. 'You know what will happen if they do.'

'I can guess.' Conway sounded as though he wanted to be sick. 'You'll protect me, Gregson?'

'I'm busy protecting myself.' Gregson bared his teeth as he guessed the result of his words on the nervous psychologist. 'Listen. There's only one way now in which we can save ourselves. What the Captain learns doesn't matter — if I am the Captain. Well?'

'Not mutiny,' said Conway weakly. 'I won't stand for mutiny.'

'Then can you get me the cards? I wouldn't dare eliminate Merrill unless I have official orders, and even if I do there's still the others to worry about.'

'Can't you eliminate them as well?'

'Yes, if I can find them.' Gregson gripped the receiver until his knuckles showed white beneath the skin, cursing the psychologist for his nervous reluctance. 'I can't order eliminations without orders from Psycho. You fixed Curtway's card, why can't you *fix* the others?'

'Curtway was an old man and due for elimination anyway. All I had to do was feed in a little false data. But the others are different. Both are young, officers, and assumed to be stable.' Conway hesitated. 'Can you give me three shifts?'

'No.'

'Two then. I can't do it in less.'

251

'Then forget it,' snarled Gregson furiously. 'Wait until Quentin sends for you.'

Gregson swore again. 'Waste! I've no time for a man who is too timid to save his own skin.'

'No.' Conway gulped, his voice echoing against Gregson's ear. 'I'll help you. What do you want me to do?'

'Meet me in the Bridge. Wait for me if you have to; spin Quentin some tale of being worried about Psycho, anything, but do nothing until I get there. *Nothing*, understand?'

'Yes, but — '

Gregson hung up before Conway could ask further questions. The man was a weakling, a cog in a machine, terrified of his own imagination and the fear of losing his life.

But he was the only one on whom, at the moment, Gregson could rely.

He sat motionless at his desk, his face heavy with thought as he tried to foresee the future. Quentin must die. That part wouldn't be difficult; the Captain was an old man and would probably collapse at the first pressure on the carotids. Conway would be willing to swear that the death had been from natural causes and, with his backing, Gregson could take over. Merrill would be quieted by promotion to the office of Chief of Psych-Police. Quieted long enough, that is, for the new Captain to arrange his elimination. Conway would have to go as well — the rest of the Council wouldn't argue — and then he could rule for as long as he managed to stave off natural death.

Gregson sighed as he thought about it, feeling some of his tension leave him now that he had a concrete plan, then glanced up in annoyance as a man burst into the inner office.

'Henderly! What's the matter?'

'This is terrible,' gasped the Chief of Medical. 'I've run all the way here from the wards. Gregson! We've got to see the Captain.'

'I know. Malick phoned me and told me about it. I'm meeting him in the Bridge.'

'Malick?' Henderly blinked. 'How did he know? I've come straight down from

Medical and haven't told anyone yet.'

'He saw the tapes,' explained Gregson. 'Something about old, white-haired men being shown on the children's viewers.' He stared at Henderly. 'That's what you were talking about, wasn't it?'

'No.' Henderly dismissed the subject as unimportant against his own news. 'It's worse than that. I've a patient in maternity, a woman, pregnant.'

'Have you?' Despite his own worries, Gregson smiled. 'Is pregnancy so rare then?'

'Of course not, but I've never known a case like this before.' He stared at Gregson. 'You don't understand. This is an old woman, one out of marriageable status. She's twenty-six years of age — and she's going to have a baby!'

Henderly sat down as if stunned by the repetition of the fact.

⋆ ⋆ ⋆

The Bridge was crowded when Gregson arrived with Henderly. Quentin sat, as he always sat, at the head of his desk, while before him Malick, Folden, Conway and a young girl sat uncomfortably on chairs. The Captain nodded as Gregson and the medical officer entered, gesturing them towards vacant seats.

'I'm glad you saw fit to come, Gregson, It appears as if we are going to have a full-scale Council meeting.'

'Are we?' Gregson looked pointedly at the girl. 'Is it normal procedure to allow Ship personnel to sit in Council?'

'Susan Curtway's my witness,' snapped Malick pettishly. 'She saw the tapes and will back up what I have to say.' He looked at the Captain. 'You laughed at me before, but this time you'll have to admit that I'm right. Those tapes must be stopped.'

'Indeed?' Quentin didn't shrug but the tone of his voice left no doubt as to how he felt. He looked at Henderly.

'I already know why you are here. You have a patient, a female, who is expecting a baby. Correct?'

'She is twenty-six years of age and should be barren.' Henderly sounded as if he still couldn't believe it. 'You know as well as I do that all females are passed through the sterilizer when they reach twenty-five, or sooner depending on the number of children they have.'

'Perhaps she missed the sterilizer,' suggested Folden.

Henderly snorted.

'Impossible! Her case history shows that she was exposed to the radiations at the correct time. My department is not at fault in this matter.' He glared at Conway. 'If you want my opinion, I'd say that the root of the trouble lies with Psycho. Malick and his tapes — and we know that Psycho issues the educational tapes on relayed channels — proves that something must be wrong.'

'It proves nothing except your own incompetence,' stormed the psychologist. 'The builders determined which tapes were to be shown when and there's nothing I can do to alter the settings. As for that woman,' he glared at Henderly, 'the mere fact that she's having a baby proves that she couldn't have been exposed to the sterility-inducing radiations as you claim. If she had, then she wouldn't be pregnant.'

'Are you doubting my word?' Anger flushed the medical officer's cheeks with red.

'I'm stating facts,' snapped Conway. He appealed to the Captain. 'You know that there's nothing wrong with Psycho, don't you?'

'I trust the builders,' said Quentin enigmatically. He looked at Gregson. 'I don't recall giving you orders to search No-Weight. Why did you do so?'

'I thought it time something was done to eliminate the Barbs.' Gregson was annoyed to find so many people with the Captain. Their presence made his plans of assassination impossible to execute and he had a sickening impression of time running out on him. 'I took it on myself to sweep out the vermin.'

'Were you successful?'

'Seven dead.'

'I see.' Quentin stared thoughtfully at the chief of psych-police and Gregson had the impression that the old man was laughing at him. 'And yet you failed, didn't you? You didn't eliminate the people the whole search was to find.' He smiled outright at Gregson's stunned expression. 'Don't look so amazed. Surely you didn't think that the Captain of the Ship was just a nominal figurehead?'

Gregson bit his lip, quickly revising his opinion of the old man. Quentin knew! He knew too much and, as he thought about it, Gregson felt a sudden fear that he might know far more than anyone had ever given him credit for. Merrill could have told him about the search, probably had, but what else had others told him? He forced himself to listen to the thin, penetrating tones as the Captain spoke.

'First, in order to allay your fears, there is nothing wrong with Psycho. You have become so used to depending on the machine that anything out of your ordinary experience is beyond your comprehension. What you have forgotten, all of you, is that Psycho is a machine built for a specific purpose. It was built more than three hundred years ago and the men who built it built it well.'

'I have never doubted it,' Conway said quickly. 'It's the others who mistrust

Psycho.' He glared at Malick and Henderly.

'And they are right to do so.' Quentin stared the psychologist into silence. 'Blind trust in the work of others can be dangerous. The builders were not omnipotent, but, aside from some tampering, the machine which we know as Psycho has operated perfectly. It is still operating perfectly.'

'You said that Psycho has been tampered with,' said Gregson thickly. 'Was that an accusation?'

'No. It was a fact.'

'Who?' Conway stared up, his face livid with fear. 'Who has dared to touch Psycho?'

'Do you really want me to answer that, Conway?' The Captain spoke to the psychologist but his eyes never left Gregson. 'Shall we say that certain men, terrified of death, had the brilliant idea of adjusting their cards so that they could not be ejected from Psycho? Shall we say that, Gregson?'

'Why ask me?' Gregson stared at the old man and felt the sweat of apprehension moisten his forehead. *Quentin knew!* Merrill? He doubted it, since the officer couldn't have known all the details. But if he had caught Curtway and the electronics man had told him what he had discovered . . .

Gregson snarled, an animal-like sound coming from deep within his throat, and his hands, as he sat hunched in the chair, hooked of their own volition into claws. Quentin knew. Therefore, in order that he could remain alive, Quentin must die.

'Merrill!'

Gregson paid no attention to the command rapped in the thin voice. Years of indoctrination fought against his survival instinct as he tried to throw himself towards the old man. Quentin was dangerous to his existence. *Quentin must die*. But Quentin was the Captain and to attack him would be mutiny. Gregson had been conditioned against even the thought of mutiny all his life and now, when he wanted to break that conditioning, he found he was unable to do so.

Suddenly Merrill was beside him. Whether he had been there all the time or whether he had stepped from some hidden room, Gregson didn't know. Hatred for the officer and what he represented burst in his tormented brain. Merrill threatened him. *Merrill had to die*.

Gregson snarled again as he lunged for the other's exposed throat.

Quentin watched them as they struggled, his face impassive, his fingers resting lightly on a row of buttons set flush with the surface of his desk. He pressed one, a panel slid aside, and Jay, together with Curtway and the remaining Barbs, entered the room.

'Separate them.'

Bosco grunted as he grabbed Merrill. Murray caught Gregson's arms and held the man until he grew calm.

'You will seat yourselves,' ordered Quentin dryly. 'If you wish to continue the battle you may do so in the proper quarter. The stadium is the place for dueling, not the Bridge.'

'I wasn't dueling,' snapped Merrill. He sneered as he looked towards Gregson, slumped over, numbed with the knowledge of his own defeat. 'Do I get his job?'

'No.'

'Why not? You promised me — '

'I promised nothing.' The whip-lash of the Captain's voice echoed around the crowded room. 'If children assume too much, must I be to blame? For that's all you are, all of you. Children. Stupid, blind, ignorant children!' The scorn and contempt in his voice lashed them to silence and they sat, like the children he had called them, listening to his next words.

'You come running to me with your petty fears and yet, all the time, the facts are before your very eyes. You plot and scheme to extend your lives, even' — Quentin glanced towards Gregson — 'toy with ambitions of ultimate power. And yet none of you has the sense or understanding or realize that, to me, all this is an old, old story. I have sat here and studied you all before. Not you, but others exactly like you. Men, lifted to a temporary power, struggling to extend that power and establish themselves as rulers of the Ship. Always I have beaten them. I always will because to me you are as glass, your motives childishly simple.

'Gregson wants to live, and who can blame him? Not I. Not Malick, whose breeding for a high survival factor is directly responsible for that laudable ambition. Conway is weak but agreed to help for mutual benefit. Merrill is ambitious, and if I was fool enough to give him Gregson's position, would be plotting against me within five years. Curtway, a good man, honest, and yet unable to see further than his nose. Henderly, a doctor, and yet a man who, like Malick, worships a machine. Jay West, one of the new generation. A man able to think and to make his own decisions, and yet even he doesn't know why.' Quentin paused and looked at the faces before him.

'It is not your fault. It is not the fault of anyone. The builders of the Ship decided, and rightly, that we must concentrate on youth at the expense of age. We have had to forge a new race, strong, moral, adventurous, to get rid of hereditary disease and physical weakness. In the Ship a man is assumed to be old at forty.

In the Ship a man *is* old at forty. Psychological training and indoctrination have seen to that. But it is wrong. At forty a man is in his mental and physical prime with generations of life still ahead. But no man at forty, within the Ship at least, can ever be wholly mature. That is why the Ship has a Captain.'

'You're old,' muttered Gregson and his eyes, as he stared at the man behind the desk, held a sick envy.

'I am old,' agreed Quentin. 'The builders knew that someone had to live past forty, to span the generations and promulgate a time-binding, long-term policy without which the Ship would have degenerated into a rabble of self-seekers. That is why there is a Captain. Not as a nominal figurehead. Not as a symbol nor as the ultimate power. But so that he can sit and watch, live and plan, not just for one generation but for others yet to come.'

'You're old,' repeated Gregson. He didn't seem to have heard what the Captain had said. 'How old?'

'There have been four Captains since

this vessel left Earth,' Quentin answered. 'The first died at sixty years of age. The second at eighty-five. The third Captain lived for a hundred and twenty-five years.' He paused, staring at their wondering expressions. 'I am over one hundred and fifty years of age.'

'Impossible!' Henderly broke the silence. 'No man can live that long.'

'No?' Quentin turned to look at the doctor. 'Why not?'

'He begins to break down,' stammered Henderly. 'His catabolism increases above his anabolism. His mind begins to get erratic. Toxins . . . body distortions . . . '

His voice trailed into silence.

'How do you know that?' Quentin stared with interested at the doctor. 'How do you know just when all this break down and senility is supposed to occur? Have you ever dissected an old man? Have you ever seen one, other than myself? Do I look as though I am in senile decay?'

'No, of course not, but — '

'But, of course, you are only repeating

what you have learned from the educational tapes.' Quentin nodded as if speaking to a child. 'Remember this. On Earth the normal life expectancy of a man or woman at the time of building the Ship was eighty years. Most people remained quite active until they were seventy, few suffered from any serious mental decay, and most remained working almost until their death. Eighty years, gentlemen. Double the normal life expectancy on the Ship.'

'But a hundred and fifty! It's incredible!'

'Why? There are no diseases on the Ship. The diet is optimum for human consumption. The temperature is regulated to within half a degree. I was born as we all were born, in a gravity double that of Earth, and I have spent most of my life near No-Weight. No strain, Henderly. No heart trouble, anxiety, neurosis, psychosomatic ills or worry about earning a living. I started life with a perfect body and have lived in a perfect environment. Why shouldn't I live to be a hundred and fifty?'

'But the Barbs,' interrupted Jay. 'We saw one who was senile, or insane, and I assume that's the same thing, at seventy.' He looked at Bosco. 'Joe, remember him? You said that he'd lived in No-Weight for thirty years.'

'In darkness,' said Quentin. 'With little water, scarce food, constant fear and endless torment. Those are the things which age a man, West. Once the mind goes, the body soon follows. The Barbs are not a good example.'

'They should be exterminated,' snapped Gregson. He seemed to have recovered himself for he looked at the strangers with undisguised detestation. 'Eliminate them!'

'Why?' Quentin seemed genuinely interested in learning the reason. 'The Barbs are valuable in that they have the highest survival factor of all the Ship personnel. They want to live so desperately that they deliberately chose the hell of No-Weight to elimination. I have fed them as best I could, contacted them, helped them in small ways. I — '

'You fed them!' Gregson half-rose to his feet then slumped as Merrill stepped

267

towards him. 'You?'

'Yes. Who else on the Ship could I trust? Who else would obey me implicitly without question and without thought of self-gain. The Barbs were valuable to me because they were the ultimate weapon against any who tried to overthrow me.' Quentin smiled at the discomforted Chief of Psych-Police. 'Call them my private army if you wish, but I prefer to think of them as one of the finest elements in the Ship.'

'That accounts for why you vetoed the suggestions for eliminating them,' said Malick. He nodded his head. 'Of course, high survival factor — it all makes sense. But what about the tapes?'

'And that pregnant woman,' said Henderly.

'Those bodies I saw in the sealed areas.' Jay flushed as Quentin stared at him. 'What about those?'

'Three questions,' Quentin said, 'and all with the same answer. Folden knows already, but how many of you have guessed at the obvious?' His eyes traveled from face to face. 'None? Not even you,

Conway? Haven't you wondered why there have been no new cards expelled from Psycho, even though many of the personnel must have reached forty during the past few shifts? No?'

'May I tell them?' Folden asked. The Chief of Supply stepped forward, his face eager. Quentin lifted one of his thin, delicate seeming hands.

'You may tell them what you told me, no more. I am interested in gauging the depth of their intelligence.'

'The position as regards supply is serious.' There was an unusual importance in Folden's voice as he spoke. 'As you all know, or should know, there can be no such thing as a perfectly balanced ecology in a closed-cycle system the size of the Ship. The very energy used in the effort of walking, for example, means energy lost. We can reclaim almost all of the water, almost all of the oxygen. I say 'almost.' There is bound to be some wastage and our reclamation units are not one hundred per cent efficient. In effect then, we started with a certain amount of essential supplies on which we have had to draw to maintain our ecology.' He paused, enjoying his moment. 'At the present rate of consumption, those supplies will be exhausted by the end of the seventeenth generation.'

'Twenty-three years,' said Henderly. 'But — '

'Please.' Quentin silenced the Chief of Medical. 'Have any of you guessed what this information means?' He waited a moment then spoke with a trace of asperity. 'Think of it. Psycho ejects no cards and so the older personnel remain alive. We trust the builders implicitly and so Psycho cannot be wrong. A woman is carrying a child, a woman who is assumed to be sterile. Obviously the sterility-inducing radiations have been cut off, and so we are going to have a tremendous increase in the birth rate. And yet, with the Ship personnel mounting by non-elimination plus increased birth rate, we know that our supplies will last no more than a few years.' He stared at them, something of his emotion breaking through his studied calm.

'Three hundred and seventeen years

ago the Ship was launched from Earth and aimed towards Pollux and a new planetary system. You have forgotten that. You have overlooked the fact that every journey, no matter how long, must eventually end.' He smiled at their dawning comprehension.

'Yes, gentlemen. Every fact in our possession leads to but one conclusion. The journey is over. '*We have arrived!*'

15

The ship was in a turmoil! Everywhere men, women and children gathered around the hastily adapted screens and stared at the black, star-shot night dominated by the glowing luminosity of Pollux. Fully twenty-eight times as bright as the Sun they had never seen, the lambent ball dominated their area of space, and speculation ran high as to just when they would be able to land on a habitable planet and escape the confines of the Ship.

Quentin knew that wouldn't be soon.

He sat in his chair behind his desk and controlled the running of the Ship as he had done for the past century and a half. He was glad he had lived to see Journey's End, glad too that now the necessity for eliminating strong, healthy men and women was over and done with. He smiled as Jay and Malick entered the room.

'Everything going to plan?'

'Yes.' Malick was almost beside himself with excitement. 'The builders thought of everything. I've been in the sealed areas examining the animals and seeds in deep freeze.' He sobered. 'The men and women too. I hope they survive.'

'They'd better,' said Quentin grimly. 'There's no one else capable of operating the investigation ships; teaching the handling and care of rocket exploration craft is something which obviously couldn't be done by means of educational tapes. We need those crews in deep freeze.'

'We need them for more than that,' said Malick. 'The cross-strains will be the making of our race!' He smiled at the Captain. 'Sorry, but I can't forget my own particular field.'

'You must never forget it. Genetics is something we must always practice. It is the only way in which we can save what we have won during the past sixteen generations.' Quentin smiled at Jay's blank expression. 'Tell him, Malick.'

'Inbreeding is dangerous,' explained

the geneticist. 'I've already told the Captain that we were approaching the breaking point by our insistence on highly-strung, intelligent people with a strong survival instinct. People like that can't live without space to move around. And, aside from that, there is another good reason why we must have an influx of new germ plasm.' Malick settled back in his chair, seeming to forget that the Captain knew all what he was about to say.

'To get a strong race, you first have to breed out all the weaknesses. You do it by inbreeding until the end product is dangerously near breakdown point, either through extreme nervous tension, as in our case, or through sterility. The remaining specimens are strong because, unless they were, they wouldn't be alive. You then cross-breed them from external stock and the results are amazing.' Malick frowned. 'At least they were with plants and animals. I only hope they will be with men and women.'

'They will be,' promised Quentin. 'A man is basically an animal.' He looked at

Jay. 'Did you understand all that?'

'I think so.' Jay frowned. 'What I can't understand is why, if the Builders had perfected suspended animation, they had to have personnel at all. Why not staff the Ship with men and women in deep-freeze, send off the Ship, and let them waken when they had arrived?'

'A good question.' Quentin nodded as if pleased. 'First, there are two ways by which men can reach the stars. One is by suspended animation as you have suggested, the other is by generation ship, which this is. We have combined both and so avoided the weaknesses inherent in either. The generation ship depends on new blood replacing the old, but the danger is that the new blood will forget what it should remember. Sixteen generations are a long time, Jay. Even with continual use of educational tapes it is still hard for some people to accept the fact that the Ship is nothing but a metal can drifting in the void. To them the Ship is the universe and they just can't imagine anything possibly being bigger.

'The deep-freeze method is just as bad.

Then the personnel have to rely wholly on automatic machinery, even as we do, but they are far more vulnerable than a generation ship could ever be. And there is another thing. We still aren't certain that they will be fertile after deep-freeze. The animals are, the men and women should be, but no one has ever rested in suspended animation for more than three hundred years before. It was a chance we dared not take.'

'I see.' Jay sat, thinking about it, trying to grasp the vast concept of which he was a part. Malick broke into his musings.

'There is another point, Jay. The people who are put to sleep on Earth and wake to find themselves on a new world, aren't really able to settle down. To them their home is Earth and, human nature being what it is, they would suffer from nostalgia. They would get homesick, long for all the things which they had left behind. We can't do that. We have never known any home than the Ship and most of us are dying to get, away from it.'

'Yes,' said Jay. He was thinking of Gregson. He put the thought into words.

'Gregson?' Quentin shrugged. 'He'll be no problem now. The pressure driving him has lifted. Once he was relieved of his morbid fear of death he reverted to normal. Now he is just as eager to explore a new planet as Merrill is.' The Captain chuckled as he stared at the young man. 'You're surprised that I let them live? Why should you be? We need men, now, Jay. Grown men who have the essential drive necessary to take a planet and twist it to our requirements. I can't afford to let what is past interfere with the main project. Merrill, Gregson, the Barbs all have their responsibilities. They know it and, knowing it, can forget small, petty grievances. After all, Jay, we bred for intelligence and intelligent men don't waste energy on trifles. They'll have plenty to occupy their time soon.'

Soon! Quentin sighed as he thought of it. First rousing the rocket crews from their suspended animation. Then three long years while the Ship orbited around the central sun. Exploration of the thirteen planets discovered by the Luna Observatories so long ago and the final testing of their theory that those planets must present a high probability of being habitable.

Then the work. The endless shuttling from the Ship down to the selected world and back again. The tests for bacteria and alien life forms. The planting of men and women as if they were seeds to see if they could survive and multiply. The isolation of the test colonies until all danger of harmful bacteria, unknown viruses and threatening ecologies had been decided. The careful cross-breeding to gain the best from the two, almost totally different races now aboard the Ship. The living personnel could be allowed to mate with whom they liked, they had already been weeded and purified in order to meet alien conditions, but the men and women in deep freeze presented a problem. They were relatively weak, still used to a single Earth gravity, still carrying within themselves hereditary diseases and slow reflexes.

Five years? Ten? A full generation? Quentin didn't know but, as he thought about it, he wished that he were a younger man. There was life and excitement and adventure ahead. Monotony and dullness and the careful fitting in of living people to the dictates of automatic machinery were all behind. It was work for a younger man, a fit, virile, eager man who would be willing to be taught and guided in the path he should take. Jay West?

Jay flushed as he felt the old man's eyes on him. He still had to fight against his inclination to stare, to wonder how any man could have lived so long, to marvel at the graying hair, the thin hands, the sunken lines on cheeks and at the corners of the eyes. He wondered if he would look like that when old.

Not that it would matter then. The children were being taught that men changed as they grew old and that the change was a normal occurrence. Still, it would be odd to see old, white-haired men and women.

'You may as well end shifts now, Jay.' Quentin relaxed in his chair, his mind made up. 'It is one of the prerogatives of the Captain to choose his own successor.

I will put it to the Council as a matter of courtesy, but there will be no doubt as to their reactions.' Quentin rose in dismissal and held out his hand, a gesture Jay had never seen before. He stared at the extended palm.

'It is an old custom,' explained Quentin. 'You may have seen it on the tapes, and then again you may have forgotten. I understand that now the tapes do include it as normal education. The idea is that you take my hand in yours, shake it, and then let it fall. The reason for the gesture is to assure you that I am your friend.'

'I see.' Jay took the proffered hand, shook it awkwardly, then let it fall. 'Like that?'

'I think so.' Quentin smiled. 'I have shaken hands only once before in my life. That was when my predecessor informed me that I was to follow his command. I thought it a good custom and decided to use it to signify my own choice.'

'Captain!' Jay blinked, still only half-aware of the implications of what Quentin had said.

'Yes. You will receive instructions from both the Council and myself. Also there are special tapes containing private instructions for the commander. I will show you those myself.' Quentin smiled. 'I must warn you not to be too impatient. The instruction is long and I have no intention of going to the converters just yet. You might be waiting for ten years, maybe longer, but you'll be learning every moment of each shift.' He sobered as he dropped his hand on the young man's shoulder. 'The responsibility is a heavy one — more now than when I took command — but you are young and adaptable and I know that you will do the best you can.'

'Yes, sir,' said Jay. He felt peculiarly humble. 'Thank you.'

He felt as if he were walking on air as he left the Bridge. The feeling lasted as he strode down the whispering corridors and into sector Five. Then, as he saw a figure before him, he faltered with sudden doubt.

'Hello, Jay.' Susan came up to him, smiling and slipped her arm through his.

'Father has told me everything. I was a fool ever to have doubted you.'

'Susan!'

'I never really believed what you said. I'm a woman, Jay, and a woman knows when a man is in love with her.' She smiled up at him. 'Did you hear the news? Genetics has given permission for free-choice marriages.' She paused, hopefully, and then shook his arm in a sudden impatience. 'Jay! Didn't you hear what I said?'

'Yes,' Jay lied. He was still thinking of what Quentin had told him in the Bridge. 'It'll take about five years.'

'What will take five years?'

'Contacting the planets.'

'Who cares about the planets?' Susan clung to his arm. 'You didn't hear what I said. Genetics has given permission for free-choice marriages for anyone who has reached marriageable status.' She looked slyly up at him. 'I shall reach full status in a few months.'

'Good,' he said. Then, as what she hinted at came home to him, he stopped, gripped her shoulders and turned her to face him.

'Susan!'

'I knew that you'd want to marry me,' she said. 'That's why I've already filed application for lowering of my status age. We can be married next month.'

Her kiss stopped his protest and, as he responded to it, he gave up.

Between Quentin and Susan, his life was pretty well planned for him as it was.

THE END

We do hope that you have enjoyed reading this large print book.

Did you know that all of our titles are available for purchase?

We publish a wide range of high quality large print books including:
Romances, Mysteries, Classics
General Fiction
Non Fiction and Westerns

Special interest titles available in large print are:
The Little Oxford Dictionary
Music Book, Song Book
Hymn Book, Service Book

Also available from us courtesy of Oxford University Press:
Young Readers' Dictionary
(large print edition)
Young Readers' Thesaurus
(large print edition)

For further information or a free brochure, please contact us at:
Ulverscroft Large Print Books Ltd.,
The Green, Bradgate Road, Anstey,
Leicester, LE7 7FU, England.
Tel: (00 44) **0116 236 4325**
Fax: (00 44) **0116 234 0205**

Charles Garrett, Special Branch's expert in terrorism, is also a victim of its effects: in an aborted assassination attempt, his wife was murdered. Now on a mission to Northern Germany to neutralize a terrorist cell led by the man who murdered his wife, his every move is blocked, and his German undercover ally assassinated. And it gets worse when he discovers a secret project that threatens the future of humanity — for he becomes the one they want to neutralize . . .

THE BLIND BEAK

Ernest Dudley

Eighteenth-century London. Blind magistrate Sir John Fielding, 'The Blind Beak', had instigated the Bow Street Runners to combat the hordes of criminals so rife throughout the city. Criminals such as Nick Rathburn, who fights his way out of Newgate Gaol. Then, by a twist of fate, Nick becomes a secret agent for 'The Blind Beak'. However, as Sir John, amid the Gordon Riots, is in the hands of the terrorising mob, Nick faces death on the gallows at Tyburn . . .

THE SECRET SERVICE

Rafe McGregor

The CIA want retired Secret Service agent Jackson back on a mission: to foil Operation Condor, a top secret plan conceived by the East German security police in the Cold War, and now in the hands of *al-Qaeda*. But he finds that he is being used as the bait in a trap. His only chance of escape is to discover who passed the plan to *al-Qaeda*. And he suspects that the answer lies in the Caribbean island of Barbados.

DARK CONFLICT

John Glasby

Simon Merrivale owns a mask and headdress, and the legend is that whoever comes into contact with them will find their body taken over by the long-dead Shaman at full moon. Merrivale is dragged from his home, and he and the relics are taken to an isolated mansion. There, Ernest Caltro and his followers prepare to conduct a Black Mass with Merrivale as its human sacrifice. Can Simon's friends Richard Blake and Stephen Nayland mount a rescue mission?

ONE STEP TOO FAR

John Russell Fearn

Claire Escott had ignored her father's warning against involvement with her fiancé, Mark Rowland. However, she little realised the extent of the scientist's corroding ambition. And it was not long after their marriage that Rowland's ruthless pursuit of a scientific empire encompassed a horrifying murder. But that was only the start of things. Mark's scientific genius and obsessive ambition to go one step further eventually led to mass destruction — and the ultimate sacrifice . . .

DR. MORELLE AND THE DOLL

Ernest Dudley

In a wild, bleak corner of the Kent Coast, a derelict harbour rots beneath the tides. There the Doll, a film-struck waif, and her lover, ex-film star Tod Hafferty, play their tragic, fated real-life roles. And sudden death strikes more than once — involving a local policeman . . . Then, as Dr. Morelle finds himself enmeshed in a net of sex and murder, Miss Frayle's anticipated quiet week-end results in her being involved in the climactic twist, which unmasks the real killer.